Diary of the War of the Pig

Diary of the War of the Pig

A NOVEL

Adolfo Bioy Casares

Translated from the Spanish by
Gregory Woodruff
and
Donald A. Yates

McGRAW-HILL BOOK COMPANY
New York St. Louis San Francisco
Dusseldorf London
Mexico Sydney Toronto

123456789BPBP798765432

Library of Congress Cataloging in Publication Data

Bioy Casares, Adolfo.
Diary of the War of the Pig.

Translation of Diario de la guerra del cerdo.
I. Title.
PZ4.B6146Di [PQ7797.B535] 863 72-4217
ISBN 0-07-073742-8

Diary of the War of the Pig

Monday, 23—Wednesday, 25 June

Since the previous Monday Isidro Vidal—the neighbors called him *don* Isidro—had stayed out of sight, scarcely leaving his room. A few of the tenants, no doubt, particularly the girls in the dressmaker's shop in the big front room, had surprised him once or twice outside his retreat. There was a lot of ground to cover in the crowded old house: to reach the bathroom you had to cross two courtyards. Confined to his room and the one next to it which his son Isidorito occupied, he was for the time being cut off from the world. The younger Vidal, explaining that he had to catch up on his sleep (he worked as a playground supervisor at the evening school on Las Heras Street), was always somehow delinquent with the newspaper his father looked forward to so eagerly, and persistently forgot his promise to take the radio to be repaired. Deprived of this antiquated contraption, *don* Isidro was therefore unable to listen to the daily fireside chats of Farrell, generally believed to be the secret chief of the Young Turks. This was a movement streaking like a shooting star through the long night of Argentine politics. In the presence of friends, who abominated Farrell, Vidal defended him, but lukewarmly; for it was regrettable, in fact, that the chief's speeches were inflammatory rather than convincing. But while condemning Farrell's lies and calumnies, Vidal could not conceal his admiration for his gifts as a speaker, for the warm tone in his voice, so profoundly Argentine; and, declaring himself impartial, he confessed that Farrell and the other demagogues had at least the merit of arousing thousands of outcasts to a sense of their dignity as human beings.

The cause of Vidal's retreat—which had now gone on too long not to be perilous—was ar unlocalized toothache and the habit of holding his hand to his mouth. One afternoon on his way back from the bathroom, he was surprised to hear a voice asking, "What is wrong with you?"

Taken aback, he lowered his hand and looked up at the speaker. It was his neighbor Bogliolo. Vidal answered politely, "Nothing."

"Why do you say nothing?" Bogliolo retorted. He was clearly acting oddly. "Why do you go around with your hand over your mouth?"

"It's a toothache," he replied with a smile. "Nothing much." Vidal was rather small and slight with thinning hair. He wore a sad expression as a rule, but when he smiled there was a sweetness about it.

The husky fellow took out a notebook, wrote down a name and an address, tore off the sheet, and handed it to him.

"Here's a dentist Go see him today. He'll fix you up like new."

Vidal went that afternoon. The dentist, rubbing his hands, explained that at a certain age the inside of the gums turn soft, as though they were made of clay. Fortunately, science had discovered a practical remedy, which was to remove the original denture and replace it with a more suitable material. After quoting an exorbitant fee, he proceeded to the drawn-out slaughter. The new teeth were finally embedded in the swollen gums.

"You may close your mouth now."

Everything went against such a move: the pain, the sensation of foreign bodies inside his mouth, the profound depression that swept over him when he faced the mirror. The next day Vidal woke up ill and feverish. His son advised him to return to the dentist, but Vidal wanted nothing more to do with him. He stayed in bed, sick and low in spirits; for some twenty hours he did not venture even to sip a *maté*. Weakness aggravated his depression, and fever gave him an excuse for staying in his room and seeing no one.

On Wednesday, the twenty-fifth of June, he made up his mind to put an end to this state of affairs. He would go to the cafe for his regular game of *truco*. Night would be the best time, he told himself, to take on his friends again.

Jimmy was the first to greet him in the cafe. (This was James Newman, of Irish descent, who knew not a single word of English. He was tall, blond, ruddy-cheeked, and sixty-three years old.)

"That's a beautiful set of choppers," said Jimmy.

Vidal stopped to talk for a minute or so with Néstor Labarthe. Néstor, it turned out, had been through the same ordeal. Opening and closing his mouth to display a row of grayish teeth, Néstor said, cryptically, "There's one drawback that it's best not to talk about."

As was their nightly custom, the boys set up their *truco* game in the cafe on Canning Street, facing the Plaza Las Heras. The expression "boys," which they all used, did not indicate (whatever Isidorito, Vidal's son, might say to the contrary) any complex and unconscious need to pass for young men; it is explained rather by the fact that once they were young and had then justifiably used the term with one another. Isidorito, who never expressed an opinion until he had checked it out with a lady doctor, would shake his head and refuse to argue the matter—as if abandoning his father to his own false reasoning. Vidal conceded that his son was right in avoiding argument: talk never leads to understanding. People are either for or against, like packs of dogs attacking or driving off a chance enemy. For instance, for each of them (when he remembered, Vidal was careful not to say "the boys"), the card game was a way of killing time, enjoyable not because the participants understood each other or were particularly congenial, but simply because they had become accustomed to it. Accustomed to the time, the place, the glass of Fernet Branca, the cards, each other's faces, the texture and color of their clothes, so used to it all that every element of surprise was eliminated. If Néstor, for example—as a gag his friends all pronounced the name with a French "r" and the accent on the last syllable—started to say that he had forgotten something, Jimmy (they called Jimmy the M.C. because of his quick mind and lively manner) would finish the sentence for him:

"Com-plate-ly."

And Dante Révora would labor the point: "You mean to tell us you've forgotten com-plate-ly?"

In vain Néstor might point out, with that face still plump as a child's, his eyes round as a hen's, speaking always in deadly earnest, that the problem had its origin in his hard-to-imagine infancy, that it was a kind of—what was the word?—fixation . . . Nobody listened. Nor would they listen when he pointed out that Dante, for instance, consistently said "chugary" instead of "sugary," and yet the latter's reputation for being an educated man did not suffer in the least.

Since the night of the twenty-fifth, when we look back upon it, will take on some of the aspects of a dream, even of a nightmare, it might be well to mention a few concrete details. The first that comes to mind is that Vidal lost every game. This is hardly surprising, since he was playing opposite Jimmy, who was totally without scruples and was cunning personified (Vidal would sometimes jokingly ask him if he had sold his soul to the devil, like Faust), and Lucio Arévalo, who had won several championships at La Paloma cafe on Santa Fe Street, and Leadro Rey, nicknamed "The Thinker." Unlike the others, Rey, a baker, had not retired, and he was Spanish-born. Though his three daughters, devoured by ambition, kept urging him to quit the business and take his ease in the sun with his friends in the Plaza Las Heras, the old man stuck to his post at the cash register. Rey was a cold man, self-centered, close-fisted, a formidable adversary in business or at the card table; but the fault that irritated the rest was a trivial one: whenever he found food within reach, even if it was merely the cheese and peanuts that were served with the drinks, his undisguised gluttony was a sight to see. "Watching him," Vidal would say, "I feel so disgusted I could wish he were dead."

Arévalo had been a newspaper man and for a while wrote a theatrical gossip column that was syndicated in the provincial press; he was the most educated of the lot. Without being a brilliant conversationalist he could express himself on occasion with a typically Argentinian brand of humor, understated and to the point, that made one forget his ugliness. An ugliness that grew more marked with the years. Ill-shaven, his glasses filmed with dust, a cigarette butt plastered to his lower lip, streaks of spittle, stained with nicotine, at the corners of his mouth, flakes of dandruff on his poncho—the complete picture of an asthmatic, long-suffering old man.

Vidal's partners in the game were Néstor, whose antics were for the most part inoffensive, and Dante, an old chap who had never been noted for his quickness of mind and who, as his deafness and shortsightedness increased, had withdrawn into his shell.

To bring that night back to life again I mention another aspect of it: the cold. It was so cold that everyone in the cafe was blowing into his cupped hands. Vidal kept looking around him, positive that a door or window must be open somewhere. Dante, who always got angry when he lost (though as a fan of the Excursionista soccer team, he should have learned to accept defeat philosophically), chided him for not keeping his mind on the game.

"The old guy's playing right into our hands," cried Jimmy, pointing to Vidal. Looking at his friend's face, with its damp, sharp, fox's nose, and the moustache which, in this icy weather, he fancied to be covered with hoarfrost, Vidal could not help wondering at his cocky manner.

"Cold weather agrees with me," Néstor declared. "So, gentlemen, batten down the hatches, there's a squall coming."

With an air of triumph he laid down a card. Arévalo recited:

> If tonight I lose my money,
> Don't wait to hear my sighs and groans;
> If I lose tonight at *truco,*
> I'll win it back at knucklebones."

"Beat that," said Néstor.

"You get the beating," said Arévalo, and he laid down a higher card.

Don Manuel, the newspaper vendor, came in, drank his usual glass of red wine standing at the bar, and walked out, leaving the door ajar as always. Ever alert to avoid draughts, Vidal got up and closed it. On the way back to his table he barely missed colliding with a skinny old woman, dressed in tatters, a living example of Jimmy's comment: "What amazing gargoyles old age can produce!" Vidal stepped aside, muttering, "Damn old hag."

We should point out, in justice, that he considered the poor woman responsible for the gust of cold air that could easily have caused an attack of bronchitis. A woman, he remarked to himself, never deigns to close a door, because she thinks of herself as a queen. Then he realized that the charge was unjust, the true culprit was the poor newspaper vendor. The old woman could be blamed for nothing besides being old. It was still possible to ask her, with barely concealed fury, what the devil she was doing in the cafe at that hour. He would have had his answer to that at once, for she disappeared through the door marked Ladies, and was never seen to come out.

They went on with the game for another twenty minutes. Praying for luck, Vidal used the classic approach: he waited patiently, and accepted everything with resignation. Don't be pigheaded, he told himself. Every intelligent player has observed that fortune favors the man who falls in step with her; to the man who crosses her she offers no support. If he didn't hold the right cards, and was stuck with partners like these, how could he hope to win? Having lost for five rounds straight, Vidal said firmly, "Gentlemen, time to break camp."

They totalled up the losses and Dante paid his team's debts and the check. The others reimbursed him, grumbling. There was the usual outcry when they saw the tip that he was leaving.

"I shall simply pretend I don't know him," declared Arévalo.

"You can't leave that," Jimmy protested.

And they all scolded him, jokingly, for being so stingy. They were talking animatedly as they went out the door, but when they faced the bad weather, the cold momentarily struck them dumb. It was drizzling and quite foggy: the street lamps were wrapped in a cocoon of mist. Somebody remarked, "This dampness is enough to rot your bones."

"It gets right to your chest," said Rey somberly.

Indeed, several of them had begun to cough. They walked along Cabello Street, heading towards Paunero and Bulnes.

"What a night," said Néstor.

Arévalo commented, with the supressed irony that was habitual with him, "Maybe it'll rain."

Dante said, "That'll cool things off," and they all laughed. Jimmy, the M.C., put it in one word, "Brr."

Social contacts are what help us most to face the trials of old age. To put it into words they themselves used, they felt hale and hearty, in spite of the adversity of the weather. Speaking half in jest, half in earnest, they kept up a cheerful, aimless conversation. The winners discussed the game; the losers, to change the subject, talked about the cold. Arévalo, who had a way of viewing a situation objectively, even when he himself was involved, remarked aloud: "Just a bunch of boys having a good time. We've never stopped being boys. Why can't the young people today understand that?"

They were so absorbed in conversation that at first they did not notice the uproar in the El Lazo alleyway. Suddenly, the yelling startled them, and only then did they notice a group of people looking expectantly in the direction of the lane.

"They're killing a dog," hazarded Dante.

"Careful," warned Vidal, "it might be rabid."

"Rats, most likely," said Rey.

Dogs, rats, and swarms of cats prowled about that alley, where refuse was dumped from the nearby market. Curiosity outweighing fear, the friends advanced a few yards. From out of the confusion of noises, distinct sounds began to emerge: curses, blows, groans, the rattle of iron and sheet metal, someone panting for breath. Out of the shadows and into the ashen light surged a gang of boys, yelling at the top of their lungs, brandishing clubs and iron bars, pounding frantically at a shapeless mass lying huddled amid garbage cans and piles of refuse. Vidal caught a glimpse of the enraged faces—obviously young, drunk with arrogance. Under his breath Arévalo said, "That—on the ground —it's the newspaper vendor, *don* Manuel."

Vidal could see that the poor old man was on his knees, his body crouched, trying to shield his battered head with his bleeding hands, trying still to hide it in a trashcan.

"We must do something," Vidal cried in a strangled voice, "before they kill him."

"Quiet," Jimmy ordered. "Don't make a fuss."

Emboldened because his friends were restraining him, Vidal insisted. "We've got to do something. He'll be killed."

Dispassionately, Arévalo remarked, "He's dead already."

"What do you mean?" asked Vidal.

Jimmy whispered into his ear, like an older brother, "Shut up."

But now Jimmy had disappeared. Searching for him, Vidal saw a couple looking on with an air of disapproval. The young man wore glasses and carried books under his arm; the girl too appeared respectable. Hoping for the moral support he had often encountered in passersby, Vidal said to them, "This is too cruel to believe!"

The girl opened her purse, drew out a pair of round-framed glasses, and, with an air of deliberation, put them on. The pair turned their bespectacled faces towards Vidal and looked at him, without expression. Carefully articulating each syllable, the young woman declared, "I am opposed to all forms of violence."

Not stopping to consider the inhumanity of this statement, Vidal tried again to rouse some fellow-feeling. "There's nothing you and I can do, but how about the police?"

"Grandpa, this is no time to be spouting off," the young man advised in a not unfriendly tone. "Why don't you beat it, before you get into trouble?"

"Grandpa" seemed quite unjustified—Isidorito had no children, and Vidal was certain that, though he was getting bald, he still looked younger than his contemporaries. It seemed to him a kind of rejection. He tried to find his companions, but failed; finally he left. He felt lost, at sea, without the boys to talk to, to share his feelings.

He reached his house, across from the automobile upholstery shop in Paunero Street. His room seemed unfriendly. Recently an uncontrollable tendency towards melancholy had altered his perception of even the most familiar things. At night the objects in his room turned into impassive and hostile witnesses. He tried to make no noise: his son, who went to bed early because he worked at the night school, was asleep in the next room. No sooner had Vidal pulled up the covers than he began to wonder in alarm if he would sleep that night at all. No position seemed comfortable, and the more his mind worked, the more he tossed and turned. (People may say what they like about mind not affecting matter.) The scene he had witnessed returned to him with intolerable vividness; he kept changing his position in the hope of driving off each image, each memory. Presently it occurred to him that a trip to the bathroom might take his mind off the subject; at least it would give him a chance of sleeping peacefully. Though he dreaded the thought of crossing two courtyards on such a wintry night, he was not going to lie awake debating whether it was necessary or not.

It always depressed him, in the small hours, to be in that unhospitable annex at the rear, cold, dark, stinking. Reasons for being depressed were seldom wanting, but why should they flood in on him particularly at this time, in this place? To blot out the memory of *don* Manuel and his murderers, he called to mind a time when—though it now seemed hard to believe—sexual experience had still been a part of his life. The high point of that other life had been the afternoon when, not knowing how it had happened, he found himself embracing a girl named Nélida. Nélida's mother, *señora* Carmen, was a cook and worked in some of the elegant family residences on the north side of town; Nélida lived with her on the second floor front, in the room now occupied by the dress shop. For some curious reason, his memory of the end of that affair coincided with another memory, painful—he knew not why—and repellent, of an old man, aroused by liquor, chasing *señora* Carmen with a carving knife. In a trunk full of odds and ends that had belonged to his parents, Vidal still had a photograph of himself and Nélida, taken in the Rose Gardens, and a faded silk ribbon she had worn. Things had changed. Time was when, if he were to come upon a woman in the bathroom, they would both burst out laughing. Nowadays he would beg her pardon and clear out in a hurry, for fear of being thought a pervert or something worse. Perhaps it was this consciousness of his lowered status that made him keep dwelling on the past. The truth was that for months now, perhaps for years, he had been living on memories; and the habit had become a vice which, like all vices, had begun as a distraction and ended by being harmful and destructive. I'll be worn out tomorrow, he thought, hurrying back to his room. In bed once more, he made this observation (with a clarity of mind that was a bad sign for an insomniac): *I've reached the time of life when weariness doesn't bring sleep, and sleep isn't necessarily restful.* Turning on his mattress he thought again of the murder he had witnessed: to relieve the distress he had felt at seeing the corpse, and at seeing it again now in his mind's eye, he fell to wondering if it had actually been the newspaper vendor. A desperate hope seized him, as if the fate of that poor wretch were vital to him; he was tempted to picture *don* Manuel alive, running through the streets, shouting out the latest headline, but he resisted the impulse, afraid of being disillusioned. He recalled the words of the girl with the glasses, "I am opposed to all forms of violence." How often he had heard that phrase without its meaning anything to him. Now, at the very moment of thinking, *What a pretentious girl,* he understood it for the first time. Suddenly he had an insight into the nature of violence, and it had the ring of truth; unfortunately, he forgot it a moment later. During nights like this, he noted, when he would have given anything to go to sleep, his mind kept working, in spite of him, at the brisk pace of a witty newspaper editorial. When the birds began to sing and the light of dawn streaked in through the shutters, he felt upset at the thought of the night he had wasted. Precisely at that moment he fell asleep.

II

Thursday, 26 June

He awoke in a fever of impatience to attend the wake. Of late, he noted, it took very little to make him impatient.

On the kerosene stove he brewed himself some *maté,* which he gulped down hurriedly, along with a few mouthfuls of bread left over from the night before. He planned his breakfast menu carefully: any extra bread or *maté* might cause a recurrence of that burning sensation which he now found to be slightly alarming. He washed his hands and feet, his face and neck, and combed his hair, first wetting it down with brilliantine and violet water. As soon as he was dressed he knocked at the door of the dressmaker's shop and asked if he might use the telephone. His false teeth had become an obsession. He could have sworn the girls were staring at him and exchanging remarks, as though he were some kind of freak, or perhaps the first man ever to have a denture. Yet strangely, even though he was watching for it, he detected not one smile, not one hint of ridicule. Their faces were serious, or preoccupied, surprised, fearful perhaps, or even angry. All of this puzzled him.

He rang Jimmy's number, but there was no answer. At Rey's, one of the girls told him her father had gone out, and not to keep calling. All this time, one of the shop girls, a fair-skinned blonde named Nélida—perhaps it was only because of the name that she reminded him of the Nélida he had known earlier—kept looking at him insistently, as if she wanted to tell him something. If that were the case, there was plenty of opportunity, since she lived in the residential part of the same building, with her friend Antonia, and Antonia's mother, *doña* Dalmacia.

It always bothered Vidal to have people looking on when he was telephoning. It upset him the way a distraction might if it occurred when he was in the midst of a difficult task. And it was even more upsetting if he was aware of not shining in the conversation. Childishness? Vidal sometimes wondered whether we learn anything with the passing of the years except to resign ourselves to our own defects. He stole a glance at the eyes that were watching him, at the flesh so close to his, at the jersey knit outlining the curve of the breasts: for anyone who admired beauty, he thought, there was nothing like youth. Suddenly an alarming thought struck him: girls that age are capable of any type of extravagant behavior while he, stuck here at the telephone, apparently understanding nothing at all, must have looked a fool. so as not to abuse the privilege of the telephone, he laid the change for his calls on the window sill and left.

He would go to the restaurant where he could talk at ease over the public telephone. Besides, he could buy a paper and find out whether it was true, as Faber and some of the others had told him, that the government pension checks were now being issued. But before leaving he made sure that the custodian (an anarchist, Galician by birth, but thoroughly naturalized, who zealously watched over the owner's interests) was not making his rounds. Luckily for Vidal, Bogliolo was not in the hallway either. Bogliolo, motivated as though by some suppressed hatred of the human race, acted as volunteer police agent for the custodian. Until around the twentieth of each month, when he usually collected his pension and could pay the rent, Vidal avoided these two with the utmost care.

How pleasant it was to walk through this part of town on a sunny morning, stretching his legs—oiling his joints, as Jimmy would say. The sky was clear and, as the boys had predicted, the cold weather persisted. The moment he stepped into the street, he noted that the upholsterer's shop was closed. Without resentment he remarked: "Not even noon, and they've already locked up. People today just don't want to work. They have it pretty soft."

He never missed an opportunity, he observed, to talk to himself, or to point out a moral.

The telephone in the restaurant displayed the usual sign, "Out of Order." Walking along Las Heras towards the square, he wondered aloud what was so special about the city today, why did it seem lovelier, and gayer? But some of the passersby were staring in a way that made him quite uncomfortable. It seemed strange that his false teeth should attract so much attention. *After all,* he reasoned, *I keep my mouth closed, and the denture is inside it, practically out of sight.* Could the new teeth, and the curious glances they occasioned, sufficiently account for his present anxiety? No, more likely it was the result of the attraction he had felt towards that young girl (perhaps she had been offering herself?), and in his own retreat from the shop, which had been more like a flight. For reasons he could not explain, he had grown more timid with the years—as though he had ceased to believe in himself and, just to be safe, was forever beating a retreat. Or was the source of his anxiety merely the fact that he was still waiting for the overdue back payments of his pension, and that money worries had become his prime concern?

He spoke to the man at the newsstand at Salguero and Las Heras in his friendliest manner, and then asked, "Where are they having the wake for *don* Manuel?"

"He's not out of the morgue yet," the man replied, in a tone that struck Vidal as quite indifferent.

"It's the weekend," he said, with a wink. "The coroner is probably enjoying a few days off and doesn't want anyone even to mention corpses."

Suddenly he sensed that the man was annoyed by his conversation, or by something or other about him, and he felt offended. The dead man had been a newspaper vendor, had he not, a colleague of this boorish young man? Did his own sympathy—expressed so tactfully and all the more commendable for coming from someone who had no connection with the newspaper business—merit such disdain? He observed that you didn't have to deserve rudeness in order to be subjected to it. But his faith in the fundamental brotherhood of man moved him to try once more.

"The wake is in Gallo Street?"

"If you say so."

"Are you going?"

"Why should I?"

"I—well, I'm thinking of going."

A little girl came up and asked for a magazine and the young lout abruptly turned his back on Vidal. At least, Vidal thought, he could avoid complete humiliation. He could leave without buying a paper. He had turned away already depressed when he heard some words that disquieted him still more.

"Some people are getting just what they've been asking for."

It occurred to him to demand an explanation, but then he thought of the young man's broad shoulders, of the muscles bulging beneath the gray jacket, and was forced to acknowledge that there were mornings now when he awoke with an aching back and a stiff spine, as though he had slept clamped in a vise. Acceptance of one's own limitations can be a rueful kind of wisdom.

He crossed the square diagonally, stopping to read the inscription on the monument. Though he knew it by heart, he never passed without reading it again. Now he felt a sudden conviction that this country of his, at the time of its early wars, must surely not have lacked a sense of close friendship among men.

From the telephone in the cafe he tried, in vain, to call his friends. At Arévalo's there was no answer. The woman next door to Néstor, who was usually willing to go and find him (provided you had taken the time to inquire about her health and the health of her family), muttered something insulting and hung up. Vidal, always interested in meteorology, observed that although the weather was milder, people still seemed to be out of sorts. Trying again to reach Jimmy, he used up his last coin. Fortunately, he thought, the phone wasn't answered by the maid, a primitive type who could barely speak and who understood nothing, but by Jimmy's niece, Eulalia.

"He's coming to see you this afternoon. I tried to talk him out of it, but he insisted."

Vidal was still thanking her for her kindness when Eulalia hung up. He went to the bakery. As he passed the El Lazo alleyway, the nightmare closed in on him again. He noted with discomfort that the lane looked just as it usually did, and that not a trace remained of what had happened. There wasn't even a policeman on duty. Had it not been for the same garbage can, he could have believed that the death of the newspaper vendor had been simply an hallucination. Vidal knew perfectly well that life goes on, leaving us behind. *But why all this haste?* he wondered. On the very spot where a few hours earlier a working man had been struck down, a gang of boys were playing soccer. Was he alone in feeling that such a thing was irreverent? It also offended him to hear these children, who regarded him with mock-innocence as well as scorn, break into a popular song:

> Here is springtime once again,
> Flowers spring from last year's dead.

He deserved some credit, he told himself, for his recent progress in the art—a passive art, to be sure—of simply not hearing taunts.

Passing by a house that was being torn down, he saw a room with no ceiling, but with its four walls still in place. *It must have been a drawing-room,* he thought.

A surprise was in store for him at the baker's: Leandro Rey was not at his post behind the cash register. Vidal inquired of one of the daughters, "Is anything wrong with *don* Leandro?"

His solicitude was not welcomed. In a high-pitched voice—perhaps she was deliberately attracting attention—twisting her thick, wet, painted lips about (as if she were tying a fancy bow on a gift), the young woman said sharply: "Can't you see there are people waiting in line? If you're not buying anything, please step to one side."

He was dumbstruck by such unjustified rudeness. To preserve his dignity, only one course seemed possible—to turn on his heel and walk out. Instead, with unbelievable calm, he waited for the power of speech to return and then gave his order. "Six brioches, four croissants, and a sugary bun."

Suppressed laughter greeted the sugary bun, as though the words had some hidden significance. No such thing. Even *don* Leandro's daughters would later admit that he had merely given his usual order. But why hadn't he simply left in dignified silence? Because he liked the pastry from Leandro's bakery. Because there were no others nearby. Because he wouldn't have to explain to his friend if tomorrow he were to ask why he hadn't bought anything at his shop. Because lately he had come to have a great respect for loyalty, loyalty to his friends, loyalty to familiar places, loyalty to the merchants who sold him food and clothing, loyalty to routine and to habit. People say that a number of explanations are less convincing than a single one, but the fact is that there is more than one reason for almost everything. And it might be that there is always something to be gained by avoiding the truth.

III

He went home to drop off his parcel. In the entrance the custodian, looking thoughtful as he leaned against his broom, was talking with Antonia, one of the girls from the dressmaker's. There was no time for Vidal to turn back before they caught sight of him, but as he went by he heard "some people . . . the least idea . . . shameless," and one complete sentence: "They don't pay their rent, but the sky's the limit in a restaurant or a pastry shop."

With the door closed behind him he felt safe at last. The man badgered him, certainly, but he was not a real bloodhound. Even the surliest caretaker today was an angel of mercy compared to the almost legendary ones he remembered from his youth; in those days you'd find yourself out on the street for the merest trifle. Besides, what the Spaniard had said was only the strict truth. Vidal and his son lived on the son's earnings (his wages from the school, and his commissions from the sale of pharmaceutical products); it never occurred to them to pay the rent until it occurred to the government to pay Vidal his pension. *It was harder for a poor man to be honest than people realized,* thought Vidal. *Harder than it used to be, and you get less credit for it.*

Now that he was in his room, relief quickly gave way to uneasiness. After so many days of fasting he felt weak; he needed something to eat. How much longer would that conversation in the lobby go on? He tried to tell himself that poverty had its advantages. For instance, it forced him into demeaning situations and schemes that were appropriate to a schoolboy, and prevented his achieving respectability, which is so closely linked to old age (*as in the case of Rey, Dante, or someone like Néstor,* he thought).

Then suddenly he heard the sound of blows, of a noisy disturbance, and the custodian and some other people shouting. With a shudder he thought of what he had seen the night before. The custodian was in a bad mood, and should be avoided at all cost. When silence fell, Vidal's pangs of hunger started up again; and hunger, overcoming prudence, drove him to leave his room. Impossible as it seemed, the custodian was no longer in the hallway. It was empty. He reached the street, turned right, and headed for the restaurant on the corner. There he enjoyed a splendid lunch of bland food he was able to chew easily with no risk of dislodging his denture. He expressed his satisfaction aloud: *It's easy to see why this is a favorite spot with the taxi drivers, who get around and know what's really good.*

On his way out he passed Bogliolo, alias Botafogo. Vidal nodded, but Bogliolo looked right through him. Vidal was still puzzling over what this piece of rudeness could mean, when his eye was caught by a gloomy but impressive sight: a row of black limousines drawn up in front of the upholsterer's. Approaching one of the shop windows he saw a number of people gathered inside.

"What's happened?" he asked.

The man in black, standing in the doorway, answered him. "*Señor* Huberman has died."

"My God, how terrible!"

Though he could barely keep his eyes open, he unhesitatingly postponed his siesta and went in to join the mourners. There were memories—and Vidal's reverence for memories exalted them until they became traditions—that linked him to the Hubermans. The thought of sharing their grief for a few moments was a comfort to him.

Poor upholsterer, with his bald skull covered with freckles, and his ears fanning out at right angles. Even his mildest quip had always amazed Vidal, who would think to himself: "It's unbelievable. To think that he can cut cloth and pile up all that money, and still find time to joke." Madelón, Huberman's daughter, was blonde and freckled too, with a cheerful disposition and an appealing little face. Vidal had courted her once, and he had not been looked on with disfavor, but eventually he cooled off: Madelón was one of those girls who are forever trying to get together a group for a game or an outing. By the time he made this discovery, he was almost one of the family. There was no risk involved, he kept telling himself, but there was something humiliating about this kind of unofficial engagement. How obstinate women could be! Whenever he addressed them, in his imagination, he would warn them not to force his hand. (Advice that fell on deaf ears—so much for the people who argue that thoughts are transmitted.) All the same, even if they hadn't forced his hand, he still would have backed out. But just because he had left Madelón so abruptly, a kind of regret still lingered with him. As we noted, she was blonde and freckled, with laughing eyes, extremely young, and though it was hard to believe now, quite pretty. During the past few years he had seen her only from time to time; she had turned into a sour, heavy-set woman, raw-boned and clumsy, and her face, grown disproportionately long, was a mass of warts and moles. As though his mind were unable to contain two such disparate images, he was always forgetting the Madelón of today, and it surprised him to come upon her as she was now. Invariably whenever he thought of her, he thought of the young girl he had known so long ago; and if he didn't give it too much thought, he could imagine that she had gone into hiding and that with a little effort he could surely find her again.

The first person he saw as he came in was today's Madelón, dumpy and commonplace. But she bore no grudge, and the moment she caught sight of him she came up and burst into fresh tears on his shoulder.

"My deepest sympathy," said Vidal. "What happened?"

In the tone of someone repeating a story for the hundredth time, Madelón told him, "The poor man was driving back along Las Heras, and when he got to Pueyrredón . . ."

"How's that?"

It seemed to him that either she was speaking in a particularly low voice, because of the circumstances, or else he must be losing his hearing.

"At Pueyrredón he came to a red light. He was getting ready to start, after the light had changed, when it happened."

"What happened?"

She explained again, and again he found himself losing a good part of the words. People don't enunciate properly any more, he thought, they talk with their mouths closed and their faces turned away from you. A little stiffly he murmured to the man on his left, "The girl doesn't enunciate properly."

"What girl?"

In a tone that was suddenly more animated, Madelón remarked, "Huguito has just left."

"Huguito?" he asked, not following.

"Huguito," she repeated. "Huguito Bogliolo."

"You mean Botafogo? We passed each other and he didn't speak to me."

"How strange! He must not have seen you."

"Of course he saw me. Just the other day he was the soul of friendliness."

"How could he not have said hello?"

"He was agreeable the other day because he wanted to play a trick on me. He'd been taken in himself, and to get even he pulled the same thing on me."

"How was he taken in?"

"The same way I was. With the denture. You hadn't noticed?"

He bared his teeth, stretching his mouth in a broad grin. Ordinarily vanity would have stopped him, in the presence of any woman, but there were exceptions.

Weariness had nearly closed his eyes when the man in black who had been stationed in the doorway came in, and there was a general movement in the room. An alarming thought occurred to Vidal: if Madelón asked him to come to the cemetery, he would have to give up his siesta. He left her for a moment, as if he were looking for someone. At the door he resisted the temptation to look back, slipped out, and went straight home.

It was so cold that in bed the blanket and the poncho over him were not enough. He had to use his topcoat too. His nerves must be in a bad way these days, he thought, if he was so depressed by the mere sight of his bed, half-covered by the brown coat, spotted and threadbare . . . But he found his siestas, on the other hand, remarkably refreshing; he could remember times when he would waken out of sorts and ill at ease. Nowadays he woke feeling momentarily rejuvenated, the way he did after a shave. But the coming of night filled him with apprehension: he knew that he would wake up in the small hours—a bad habit—and begin to think sad thoughts.

He slept for a half hour. Heating water for his *maté,* he reflected that in the course of a lifetime, however short, we are two or three people in succession: for instance, he had first been a man who liked his *maté* bitter, next a man who would not touch it because it disagreed with him, and now he had acquired a taste for *maté* with sugar. He was just about to pour boiling water over the leaves when Jimmy walked in. Could it be the cold, he wondered, that had sharpened Jimmy's nose and chin, turning his face into a fox's muzzle?

It was a well-known fact that Jimmy's intelligence was joined to an almost animal instinct: whenever you were about to eat, he was certain to pay you a call. Now he strode in, laid one hand boldly on the sugary bun, and the other on the *croissants.* After a moment's irritation, Vidal congratulated himself: all that pastry, which he had bought in the childish hope of gaining back his strength, usually caused all kinds of upsets in his digestive tract.

After sipping first on the *maté*—with other people this was merely ritual courtesy, but with Jimmy it was a commonsense precaution—Vidal asked, brewing a second time, "Where is the wake?"

"Whose wake?" asked Jimmy, as though he had not understood. But he did not seem in the least absent-minded, rather he seemed intent, like a card-player concentrating on the game.

"The newspaper vendor," said Vidal patiently.

"That's a cheerful thought."

"Think of how he was killed. Surely some show of loyalty is called for."

"Better lie low."

"And our loyalty?"

"That comes later."

"And what comes first?" demanded Vidal, a little annoyed.

"What comes first? This mania of yours for going to every wake and every funeral. You've reached the age when people start making the graveyard their clubhouse."

"Shall I tell you something? Today I slipped away from the Hubermans' just to avoid going to the funeral."

"That doesn't prove a thing. You probably wanted your nap."

Vidal did not answer. It was no use to try to hide his thoughts from Jimmy. He clapped him on the shoulder. "Want to know something? What woke me this morning was my impatience to find out where the wake was going to be."

"Impatience is another story," remarked Jimmy, unrelenting.

"What do you mean?"

"Impatience and anger are always with us. Think of this war, for instance."

"What war?"

Turning a deaf ear, Jimmy went on. "At a certain age . . ."

"That expression turns my stomach," Vidal warned him.

"Mine too. Still, there's no denying that at a certain age people begin to lose control."

"What control?"

Ignoring the question, Jimmy continued, "People just get

flabby all over, they lose their grip on things. You want evidence? Everywhere you look, the first arrivals are always the old people."

"You're right," Vidal admitted, impressed. "I'm not old yet, but I've come to that stage."

"In short, it makes a bad combination: impatience and slow reflexes. It's no wonder they dislike us."

"Who dislikes us?"

Instead of replying, Jimmy asked him, "How do you and your son get along?"

"Perfectly. Why do you ask?"

"Néstor's the one who's really well off. He and his son are like brothers."

The words struck a chord: Vidal embarked on one of his pet theories. Having stated his premise—"Keep your distance, then you know where you stand" (a phrase which on this occasion did not meet with the usual approval)—he felt himself stimulated by the opportunity to exercise his powers of thought and expression, sharpened by long experience; but he was suddenly disturbed by the idea, at once rejected, that he had already expressed these same ideas to Jimmy, in the same words. "It's a law of nature," he began gloomily, "that parents go before . . ."

Abruptly Jimmy cut in. "What time does your son come home?"

"He'll be here any minute," Vidal answered, concealing his mortification at being interrupted.

"I'm going right now before he sees me."

The words came as a disagreeable surprise. Vidal started to protest, but checked himself. He was sure he was not blinded by affection; his son was a generous, likable young man.

IV

VIDAL crossed the two courtyards to the washrooms. Nélida was there, doing a laundry in one of the washtubs and talking with Antonia and Bogliolo's nephew. Antonia was petite, with chestnut hair, coarse skin, and short arms; her voice, low-pitched and toneless, was the voice of one just awakening. But she had many admirers in the building. Bogliolo's nephew—tall, thin, beardless, round-eyed, wearing a shirt through which the undershirt could be clearly seen—put his arm around her waist and said, "You're a real prize!"

There's nothing like youth, thought Vidal. *There's probably something going on between those two.*

"What were you two talking about?" he asked.

"Go away, go away," cried Antonia, laughing.

"You're throwing me out?"

"No, of course not," Nélida assured him.

Antonia insisted. "But we can't have *don* Isidro listen to what we're saying."

Vidal noted that the pupils of Nélida's eyes were flecked with green.

"Why not?" protested the young man. "*Señor* Vidal is still young in heart."

"Open-minded," added Nélida.

"I try to be," said Vidal. It was his lot, he thought, to live in a period of transition. In his youth, women had not spoken with anything like the freedom they did now.

"It's not merely that he's young in heart," Nélida insisted. "*Señor* Vidal is in the prime of life."

Too bad she calls me señor, thought Vidal.

"What year were you born in?" Antonia asked him.

He was reminded of the time when two young women had come to the building, making a survey for some psychological or sociological institute. *Next,* he thought, *this one will be pulling out her pen and her notebook.* And then he reflected: *How I enjoy being with young people.*

Jokingly he told her, "That's a question one doesn't ask."

"You're right," agreed Bogliolo's nephew. "Pay no attention to her. I may as well tell you, Faber wouldn't answer her either."

"You're not comparing *señor* Vidal with that old fossil," cried Nélida, with unexpected warmth. "Why, he must be fifty at least."

I'd put him between sixty and seventy, Vidal thought. *For these youngsters a man is old at fifty.*

Nélida kept it up, almost aggressively. "It's my guess *señor* Vidal is younger than your uncle."

The supposition was not to the young man's liking: his face darkened, and his usually apathetic expression was replaced by one of open hostility. Vidal could not help thinking that this rather childish show of affection for a rather detestable relative was to the boy's credit. And he wondered at the same time whether he would have the courage to go into the bathroom while these young people were here. His embarrassment was ridiculous, because after all . . . adolescent timidity, that's what it was. At heart every man is a boy disguised as a grownup. Were all the rest like that? Was even Leandro Rey a boy too? Very likely he was deceived by Leandro, as the others were deceived by Vidal himself.

V

For a timid man life is an obstacle course. Starting back to his room he thought that a man going into a bathroom is at least a little less ridiculous than a man who lacks the courage. Can anything be more shameful than to let it appear that one is ashamed? And to make matters worse, the incident was not closed: there was no doubt that he would shortly have to go back. His only hope was that the girls and Bogliolo's nephew would have gone. His hand was on the doorknob when he was surprised by Bogliolo, asking, "How are you feeling, *don* Isidro?"

With a fellow like this you never knew where you stood. In his confusion Vidal answered, "And how are you, *don* Botafogo?"

He hoped the man had not heard the nickname, which he tried to smother as it formed on his lips.

Bogliolo stared down at him. He spoke very solemnly. "I'm taking the liberty of giving you some advice, like a father speaking to his son. The Spaniard is putting the pressure on. So pay your rent, before he makes a scene. You know how people are. They're saying you live it up in restaurants and won't pay for the roof over your head."

He stalked off, but turned back to add, "Don't ask me how, but they even know what you paid for the denture."

Returning to his room, Vidal found his son putting things away in the wardrobe. "Straightening up?" he asked.

With his back still turned, the boy gave a grunt that Vidal

construed to mean *yes*. He looked on, not heeding, as Isidorito put away his father's old slouch hat, his scarf, his razor and razor strop, and the little wooden chest marked *Souvenir of Necochea* in which he always kept his pocket watch at night. Suddenly Vidal came to.

"Say, those are my things. I want them out."

"They're handy," said Isidorito, closing the wardrobe.

"What are you doing? The hat, the scarf—all right. But if I want to know the time tomorrow morning, it's no good having my watch in there."

"Tonight the Youth Group of the 21st is meeting here."

Vidal thought he detected behind these words a trace of impatience or irritation.

"That's fine," he exclaimed with sincerity. "I'm glad you're bringing your friends here. Besides, I don't know—it seems to me so much better for you to be with people your own age."

He checked himself in time, he had no wish to reproach his son. When he forgot himself he would aways bring up the subject of that woman doctor who had brought out something pedantic and aggressive in the boy's character. As if he sensed a veiled attack on her, Isidorito answered gruffly, "I could do all right without them."

"You ought to have seen the way my father welcomed my friends. Within his modest means, of course. He would even insist that mama change into her best dress, after the *empanadas* were fried."

"What a mania you have for raking up the past."

"They were your grandparents, after all."

"I know perfectly well we come from simple folk. You keep reminding me every other minute."

Vidal glanced at his son with a mixture of curiosity and affection. Even those who are nearest and dearest to us, he told himself, have thoughts we can never guess. "We don't wear our hearts on our sleeves," was the way he expressed it. There had been a time when he thought of this attitude as a kind of shield, defending the individual freedom of every human being; but now it saddened him to see the loneliness it could lead to. Trying to get through to his son, to draw him out of his isolation, he said, "Anyway, *I'm* glad they're coming. Only just now I was thinking how I always enjoy myself with young people."

"Nobody understands why."

"You don't enjoy them yourself?"

"Why shouldn't I? I'm not you."

"Oh, I see—it's the generation gap. We don't understand each other. I suppose the doctor explained the whole thing?"

"Look, that may be, but it really would be better if the boys didn't find you here. Especially since one of them is a real fanatic. A very popular guy, he drives a produce truck. He's a real character, a kind of popular hero. They've even made up a song about him:

> Move off the corner
> You crazy free-wheeler . . ."

"And I'm supposed to walk the streets while you entertain your friends?"

"Don't be silly! Walk the streets? I wouldn't want anything to happen to you."

"I can't believe my ears. You plan for me to hide under the bed?"

"You're talking nonsense! I've got a better idea." Taking his arm, Isidorito led him outside. "Let's not waste time. They'll be here any minute."

"Don't push. Where are we going?"

Isidorito winked and laid a finger to his lips, hushing him. "To the attic," he whispered.

This could have been understood as either an explanation or as an order. In the first courtyard they passed Faber, on his way to the bathroom. They saw Nélida too, carrying a pile of laundry. With his son at his heels, Vidal hurried up the little stairway, hoping the girl had not seen him. Up above he had to crawl in on all fours since the roof was so low.

"You'll be quite comfortable here," Isidorito assured him. "If you stretch out on one of these chests, you could even take a nap. Turn out the light, and don't come down till I call you."

Before he could protest, Isidorito had vanished. To Vidal the place seemed ill-chosen. *Don* Soldano, the wholesale dealer in eggs and poultry, used it as a storeroom. It was piled high with filthy, stinking crates; and with the lights off, the darkness was intolerable. Isidorito had hurried him so that he had forgotten to bring his poncho or his coat. In a way this was all to the good, because he would certainly have had to take either to the cleaner's; on the other hand, he was shaking with cold, and the floor felt as hard as rock. He should at least have stopped at the bathroom before coming up . . . He always lost his composure when his son became impatient.

He had felt equally helpless twenty years earlier with the boy's mother. Violeta was an overpowering woman, with strong convictions on every subject and never the slightest need for supporting evidence. In the face of such assurance he had always felt that any doubts he might have would be offensive, and for a long time he allowed himself to be dominated. What images came first to his mind when he looked back on his life with Violeta? Above all else, monumental curves of pink flesh, and the color of her hair—reddish blonde—and an acrid odor, the scent almost of a wild animal. Next a series of episodes from a period which, in retrospect, seemed to have passed quickly. The day she announced to him—in the Palais Blanc Theater—that she was expecting a child and they would have to get married. The day the child was born. The day he found out at last that she was deceiving him. Because they were showing a film with Louise Brooks, he had gone to the Palais Blanc, and suddenly recognized an odor that filled him with longing; and then in the darkness, in a row ahead, a voice about which there was no mistaking: "Don't worry, he never goes to the movies without me." . . . The day he had found Violeta's note on the pillow: she was entrusting the child to him—"You're a good father, etc."

—and was leaving, heading up the Paraná River with a Paraguayan. And so he had found himself—and he wondered if the fault was not partly his—in a situation that was frequently celebrated in the lyrics of tangos but, judging by what he saw around him, was not at all common in everyday life. When Violeta left him, his friends talked of nothing but how they themselves longed to shake off the marriage yoke, as though their wives were a burden laid across their backs. Violeta's infidelity was a vexation, but it did not cause him the pain and despair people suppose to be inevitable. And the way he cared for his child gained him enormous prestige among the women of the neighborhood. (Although there was one who assured him roundly she could never respect a man who would stoop to domestic chores of that sort.) All this seemed to prove that other people felt very differently about things . . . It was about this time that he decided to move to an apartment (a relative had died, leaving him a small sum—how that would have upset poor Violeta if she had found out). But as he had neighbors where he was to take care of Isidorito while at work, he gave up the idea. The money dwindled away in routine expenses, and he ceased to think about moving . . . Next he recalled the afternoon he had come home to hear, above the voices of keyed-up women, the appreciative comment of one of them: "Just look at his little thing." The effect of this memory was to make him want again to go to the bathroom. He was really desperate, but he dared not climb down after being told not to. In obeying his son so blindly he was acting like a pathetic old man; but this, he told himself, was the reasoning of a spoiled child—Isidorito surely had some good cause for telling him not to go back downstairs. But one thing was certain: he could not hold off any longer. As well as he was able, he dragged himself across the stinking attic to the farthermost crates and, balancing unsteadily on his knees, urinated interminably. He had nearly finished when he noticed streaks of daylight between the floorboards: *señor* Bogliolo's room must be directly underneath. This was a terrifying thought: he dreaded the very thought of an argument in this place littered with chicken droppings. With infinite precautions he managed to conceal himself in the pile of cartons at the opposite end of the room. A moment later he was dreaming about a man who had hidden in an attic during the Rosas dictatorship, until he was betrayed by the oldest of the children he had begotten in these years of concealment, and was beheaded by the tyrant's hired assassins. Later—but it was all part of the same dream—he was leaping hurdles on horseback, covering himself with glory while the women looked on, and explaining, in a blend of personal modesty and patriotic pride, "Naturally I can ride a horse, can't any Argentine?" But, never having been in the saddle before, he suddenly lost confidence in his horsemanship, and ended by taking a painful spill. Nélida, smelling of lavender, was bending over him, asking, "Are you hurt?"

No, what Nélida was actually saying was, "They've gone."

"What time is it?" he asked. He was still half asleep.

"Two o'clock. They've left. Isidorito didn't come because he had to walk a few blocks with them, but he won't be long. You can come down now, *don* Isidro."

When he tried to stand up his whole body ached, and he felt a stab of pain in the small of his back. *Another attack of lumbago?* he wondered. It humiliated him that the girl should see the difficulty he was having (in his mind the term was *miseries*). He tried to make excuses. "I must seem like an old cripple."

"You were in a cramped position."

"A cramped position," he agreed, but without conviction.

"Let me help you."

"Absolutely not. I can manage."

"Please let me."

Unaided, he could never have got out of the place. Nélida, supporting him like a trained nurse, helped him back to his room. He gave in to her, unresisting.

"Now let me help you get into bed."

He smiled at her. "No, we haven't quite come to that yet. I can get to bed on my own."

"All right. I'll wait. I'm not going until you're in bed."

Looking at her as she stood in the middle of the room, with her back to him, he observed that she had everything one could hope for in a fine-looking female. He managed to undress and climb into bed.

"I'm ready," he said.

"Do you have any tea? I'll make you some."

He felt blissful, in spite of the lumbago. For years—he could not recall how many—he had not been pampered this way. He was about to discover, he thought, the comforts of infirmity and old age. Pouring the tea, Nélida said she would stay with him a bit longer; she sat at the foot of the bed and talked to him—just to be making conversation, he thought—about her life, and told him, not without a hint of pride, "I have a fiancé. A young man I'd like to introduce to you."

"Certainly," he answered, without enthusiasm.

He was thinking how he liked Nélida's hands.

"He works as a mechanic, in a garage, you know. But he's very talented and he plays guitar in a folk trio that performs every night in the cabarets downtown, and especially around Plaza Italia."

"When are you getting married?"

"As soon as we've saved up enough for the apartment and the furniture. You have no idea how much he loves me. I'm everything to him."

She went on talking. To hear her, one would suppose her life was an endless round of parties and dances, at which she was the presiding belle. Vidal listened with unbelieving tenderness.

The door opened, and Isidorito stood looking at them in surprise. "I'm sorry, I didn't mean to interrupt."

"Your father didn't feel well," the girl explained. "I thought someone should stay with him until you got back."

It seemed to Vidal that Nélida had blushed.

VI

Friday, 27 June

He felt better in the morning, but not so much so that he was not still slightly uneasy. If he had money, he thought, he would go to the pharmacy, have an injection, and be as good as new (if not that very day, then at least by the end of a week, after the entire series of shots). But until he collected his pension, any expense which was not absolutely necessary was out of the question. If *señor* Garaventa waited on him at the pharmacy, there would be no problem, since men understand problems of this kind; but with *doña* Raquel things would get complicated. On the other hand—and this made it even more difficult for him to decide—*doña* Raquel had skillful hands, while *señor* Garaventa was known to be a real butcher.

On his way to the bathroom he ran into Bogliolo, who, gesturing nervously, was relating something to Faber. Turning to Vidal, Faber asked him, "And you, where were you hiding last night?"

Vidal hesitated for an uncomfortable moment. At last he stammered, "Well, the fact is . . ." It was not necessary to go on.

"As for me," Bogliolo began again, "even though it's not easy to catch me napping . . ."

Vidal glanced at him curiously: he was talking strangely, and his manner was altogether different.

Raising his voice, Faber succeeded in recapturing their attention.

"I managed to take cover in a men's room," he explained, "but, believe me, it was a night right out of a novel. There was one moment when they knocked on the door and I thought my last hour had come. But they left."

"As for me," said Bogliolo once more, "though it's not easy to catch me napping, I found myself surrounded by a swarm of kids. But I kept my head, and decided I'd better go along with things."

"At dawn," Faber went on, "when at last I could see my way clear, I couldn't stand. From sitting so long I'd got a touch of lumbago, or maybe twisted my back."

"Exactly what happened to me," cried Vidal, carried away by a fraternal impulse.

"I doubt it," Faber protested. "Why, after I came out, I was bent double for hours."

In spite of his ineptness in expressing himself, Bogliolo managed to silence them and go on with his story. "The boys played along with me, and we went on talking, making plans for the next attack, until it got very late. Don't think I wasn't in a tight spot: I was acting cool as a cucumber, but I was damned nervous. When the meeting broke up I wanted to stay here, but they insisted I go with them. I wanted to stick with your son's group, because after all I know him. But two of them took me by the arm and we walked for hours, talking like real friends, out Santa Fe towards the Pacific Bridge. When we got to the Giol Wine Company warehouse one of them—the one they call Babe—told me to forget everything I'd heard that night. But his tone of voice was the same, as friendly as ever. The other one admired my denture, and suddenly yanked it right out of my mouth, pretending that he wanted to get a good look. You won't believe this, but when I asked to have it back, the shorter of the fellows told me to head home in a hurry if I wanted to make it in one piece."

"Anyway we came off better than Huberman," Faber remarked.

With the stiff manner he always assumed when he was broaching a touchy subject, Bogliolo ventured to say, "*Don* Isidro, your son strikes me as a dependable young man. Do you feel up to sounding him out?"

"Sounding him out?"

"Getting him to find out the lay of the land, whether I have any chance of recovering it. You know what a denture costs?"

"You're asking me?"

"May I count on you?"

"Of course, of course. But what happened to Huberman?"

Bogliolo raised his eyebrows, hesitating. "The poor man was driving along Las Heras . . ."

Faber moved him a bit to one side, and broke in. "May I speak? I cut out the statement of the accused from the paper." He drew a clipping from his pocket and carefully unfolded it. "They get right to the point. Listen to this:

" 'The moment I saw that bald skull in the car ahead, I realized I had picked the wrong lane. I'll admit I may have been prejudiced, irritated in advance. But believe me, gentlemen, everything happened just as I had foreseen it would. When the other cars started up, the one ahead of me just stayed there, while that bald old codger sat there, waiting for his reflexes to wake up so he could get going. The old man was the victim of resentment that's been building up inside me for a long time, because I've been in the same spot so many times, with the same kind of old man. I couldn't help myself. The temptation to fire at that bare skull of his, dead center between those spreading ears, was too strong for me.' "

"What did they do to that lunatic?" asked Vidal.

"Come, come," protested Bogliolo, "that's no way to look at it."

"He was released immediately," Faber answered.

Bogliolo turned on the faucet over the wash tub and drank, cupping the water in his hand. "Please, don't forget," he asked again, "to sound out your son."

Bogliolo went back toward his room. The other two followed slowly.

"I feel sorry for him," said Faber.

"I don't, not in the least."

"It's just a way he has, he's not a bad sort really. It's just that the poor devil is under the landlord's thumb. He doesn't know which way to turn."

They came upon Nélida and Antonia. Vidal noticed that neither of them greeted Faber. Faber left.

"Permit me to congratulate you on your acquaintance, *don* Isidro," said Antonia, sarcastically.

"You mean Bogliolo?"

"Never mind Bogliolo. No, it's that other old villain I can't stand."

"Antonia's quite right," Nélida declared.

Looking at her, Vidal admired the graceful curve of her throat: hers was really a swanlike neck, he thought. He was always finding some fresh marvel in this girl. Quickly he asked, "What has he done?"

Antonia's voice was savage. "What hasn't he done, that disgusting old man? Just thinking about it makes me furious. At night he comes out with the dirtiest propositions, hanging around the washrooms the way he does. If you don't believe me, ask Nélida."

"From ten o'clock on, he's always on the prowl," Nélida said.

"I can't believe it."

"It's the absolute truth," said Antonia. "Nobody knows it better than we do."

"What are you saying? Doesn't he realize what he's doing? He must be so desperate that he's lost all self-respect." He admitted that Faber's conduct was incredible and could not be too strongly condemned.

"I'd turn in an old man like that without a qualm," Antonia declared.

Vidal fully agreed with her, but added: "The poor devil." He said it several times, and tried to put up other defenses against Antonia's merciless attack.

"Old men like him shouldn't be allowed to live, not one of them."

"True. You're perfectly right. Old men who get mixed up with young women are a sorry spectacle. Disgusting. You're right. Absolutely right. But still, compared to an informer, a traitor, a murderer . . ."

"You're not the injured party. Put yourself in my place."

"Certainly he offended you. Faber's behavior is unforgivable. But perhaps the poor fellow can't admit how repulsive he is, because if he did, it would mean admitting he was old and approaching death."

"What does that have to do with me?"

There was no answer to this question, but feeling he should make one last effort on Faber's behalf, Vidal summed up his defense. "Granted, everything you say is quite true. He's old, he's ugly—but we can't hold that against him. Nobody's old and ugly from choice."

Antonia looked at him, shaking her head, as though what she had been listening to made no sense. But she would overlook it simply because she accepted him for what he was.

"There's no use talking with *don* Isidro. Well, I'm going to do a bit of laundry."

Before following her, Nélida whispered to him, "You mustn't talk like that when Antonia's around."

VII

HE felt much better. A long day spent lounging around his room had effected a remarkable improvement. If he did not go out, it was only because Nélida advised against it. At noon, as he was about to go to the restaurant, he met her at the entrance.

"Don't go out," she said. "I think that going out into the street would be very unwise. Take a rest today, and tomorrow you'll feel fine."

"But you can't live on air. And believe me, today I don't even feel equal to boiling noodles."

"My aunt Paula brought me some small pastries. Will you let me share them with you?"

"If you'll come and eat them with me."

"No, I can't. Please, don't be offended. You know how people are."

He ate one of the pastries, then a second, and finally a half-dozen—they were really delicious—washing them down with *maté*. Nonetheless they weighed heavily on his stomach, and he took a long nap, of the sort he used to have in the old days, from which he would waken in a daze, not knowing whether it was noon or the middle of the night. He made more *maté,* waited in vain for Isidorito to bring back the radio, which he had finally taken to be repaired, resignedly boiled some noodles, which he ate with grated cheese, leftover bread, and red wine. When nothing remained but crumbs, Jimmy walked in.

"Am I late?" he asked.

"Incredible as it seems, yes. There's nothing left."

"You don't mean to tell me you haven't got some dessert in the closet? A pudding? Or at least a chocolate bar?"

"Well, there's Isidorito's chocolate. It'll sit like lead on your stomach."

"Don't worry, my digestion is fine," said Jimmy, already gnawing on the chocolate. "I hope this won't cause any trouble between you two. That reminds me, tonight we're playing at Néstor's. Néstor and his son get along fine, that makes it safer for us. Are you coming?"

Vidal thought he could accept. Nélida would not know, and it would do him good to be with the boys, to get some fresh air and shake off the gloomy thoughts that had been pressing in on him during his long day of rest and indigestion.

"Is it cold out?"

"Button up tight. Funeral wreaths are expensive right now."

Vidal threw his poncho over his shoulders and they went out into the night.

"What's wrong with you?" Jimmy asked him. "You're bent double."

"Nothing much. A pain in my middle."

"It's the years, old man, the years. A man, if he's smart, prepares himself well ahead of time. If he thinks about old age, he loses heart, you can tell, and people say he's given up before the battle. If he doesn't think about it, they remind him to act his age and point out that there's no fool like an old fool. There's no defense against old age. Look, there's a bunch of people gathered at the corner, a street gang perhaps, or maybe one of those so-called repression squads . . . It'll be just as easy to turn the corner here and avoid them."

"A person learns to put up with everything. Do you suppose that in our young days two elderly Argentine gentlemen would have resigned themselves to taking such precautions?"

"Oh, in those days everyone seemed sterner. But who knows what they all were like when no one was watching?"

VIII

Néstor lived with his wife and son (also named Néstor) on Juan Francisco Seguí Street in a small house consisting of a dining-room and a front room facing the street, and another room together with the service quarters at the rear, overlooking a garden or a yard. When Vidal and Jimmy arrived, the others were already gathered in the dining-room. On one wall hung a pendulum clock, stopped at twelve. Néstor's wife, *doña* Regina, never appeared when her husband entertained his friends; in response to any inquiry about her, Néstor would nod vaguely towards the rear of the house.

"They're expecting me," his son was saying, "in a cafe across the avenue."

"Avenue Alvear," Dante explained.

They all laughed. Jimmy said solemnly, "Our old friend here is pre-historic."

"*Señor* Dante meant to say Avenida del Libertador," said Néstor's son politely.

"Actually Dante's quite right," said Arévalo. "We ought to put a stop to this business of changing names. Every twenty years the houses change, the house numbers change, the name of the streets change . . ."

"And the people change," Jimmy put in, and he began to hum "*Where has my Buenos Aires gone?*"

"You wouldn't even believe you were in the same city," said Arévalo.

The young man said goodnight to his father's guests. Vidal apologized.

"What a way for us to take over your house."

"We're forcing you out," said Arévalo.

"The important thing is that you feel comfortable," the young man replied. "Don't worry about me."

"But it's outrageous that you should have to leave on account of us," said Arévalo again.

"What does it matter?" protested the young man. "I'm on the side of my father's friends." And he added, stammering, "Come what may."

He patted his father's shoulder affectionately, smiled, waved a hand, and left.

"A fine boy," said Vidal.

"A phoney," Jimmy muttered.

Néstor served Fernet, peanuts, and olives. Rey stretched out his hand greedily. They drew lots. Luckily for Vidal he had Jimmy and Arévalo as partners, so tonight, even before they began, the outcome was a foregone conclusion.

"What can you tell me about the upholsterer?" asked Rey, with his mouth full.

"Did you know him?" Vidal asked Néstor.

"I've seen him a thousand times across from your place."

Athough Néstor pronounced *your* with an "r" that was distinctly French, no one smiled. Except Jimmy, who not only grinned, but winked.

"Who are you talking about?" Dante wanted to know.

"I've been noticing an alarming change," declared Arévalo.

"About Rey's grandfather," Jimmy told Dante, suppressing a laugh.

"I don't believe you," retorted Dante.

"I've been noticing an alarming change," Arévalo persisted. "We used to read in the papers about things like this happening to persons we didn't know. Now it's happening to people right in the neighborhood."

"People we know," added Rey, indignantly.

"One step further and heaven help us," groaned Jimmy, with a wink.

"You have no feelings," said Rey, as if to discredit him. "In the first place, why does the government permit this charlatan to spread his poison over the radio?"

Vidal said thoughtfully, "I think Farrell has made our young people conscious of themselves. If you're against the fireside chats, it amounts to admitting that you're just one of the fogies."

"What kind of reasoning is that?" asked Arévalo, with a smile.

"You see?" Rey asked them. "You see how the poison works? Here's our own friend using the demagogue's terminology."

"I agree," Arévalo conceded. "But you go too far the other way, Leandro. You're too conservative."

"Why shouldn't I be?"

"Why do old people arouse such hatred?" retorted Arévalo. "Because they're too self-satisfied and they won't make way for young people."

"Who, for instance, is going to budge 'The Thinker' from his cash register?" Jimmy asked.

"Shall I make way for incompetents, just because they're young? Give up all I've worked for? Just hand over the reins?"

Jimmy winked at the others and sang: "*The years go grumbling by.*"

"Joke about it if you like," said Néstor, "but if the authorities don't put a stop to it, who's going to be safe?"

"Remember the rich old lady on Ugarteche?" Rey asked them.

"The old woman with all the cats?" asked Arévalo.

"Yes, the old woman with the cats. What could anyone have against her? She had one eccentricity, feeding cats. Well, yesterday, at the corner near her house, a gang of young ruffians beat her to death with their fists, in full view of the passersby, who did nothing."

"And of the cats," said Jimmy, who could never endure painful subjects for very long.

"They were sniffing at the body," Rey said.

Jimmy remarked to Vidal, "When Rey's talking to you, you need an umbrella. Did you see that last piece of peanut go flying by? We old folks spit when we talk. Up to now I thought I was safe, but now I've begun too. A few days ago, I was talking to somebody and in the heat of the conversation some spittle landed on his sleeve. To keep his attention I went on talking, but all I could think of was please don't let him notice."

"The case of the granfather is even worse," said Arévalo.

"You mean Rey's grandfather?" asked Dante.

"Don't any of you read the papers?" demanded Arévalo. "He was a burden to the family, and was liquidated by his two granddaughters, aged six and eight."

"Respectively," Rey explained.

"Are you deliberately trying to upset me?" Jimmy asked them. "Let's talk about serious matters. Is River going to win the soccer game on Sunday?"

"When honor is at stake the River team surpasses itself," Rey stated.

Dante asked peevishly, "What does that have to do with Rey's grandfather?"

They spoke of extraordinary incidents that had occurred both on the playing fields and in the grandstands.

"Nowadays," Rey declared, "a sensible man watches soccer in front of his television set."

"For my part," said Dante, who had understood for once, "I don't go to the stadium any more, even if the Excursionists are playing."

Néstor, declaring himself in favor of seeing "real games, first hand," announced, "I'll be in the grandstand Sunday, rooting for River."

"Don't be idiotic," implored Jimmy.

"Sheer suicide," said Rey, phlegmatically.

Dante explained, "Néstor's going with his son."

"Well," said Rey, "that makes all the difference."

Expansive in his paternal pride, Néstor explained: "You can see for yourselves. I know quite well what I'm doing, and I've no desire to commit suicide. My boy's going with me."

"All this while, with all the talking," said Jimmy, "he's holding up the game and putting off defeat. Could it be the old rascal is sandbagging us? Maybe he's a real shark."

After four games the losers begged for mercy. Dante announced his intention of going to bed early; Néstor offered a last round of Fernet and peanuts. It was midnight, Rey remarked. They settled their debts.

"We ought to be extraordinarily lucky in love," said Néstor.

"Why?" Jimmy asked. "It wasn't because of the cards you held that you lost."

Rey smiled and shook his head. In a tone of friendly reproach he said, "At least spare us our illusions."

"Look at him," said Arévalo. "All of a sudden his arrogance is gone. People are right in saying the mere idea of love makes us more human."

They left together, but each one quickly took off in his own direction, except for Rey, who said to Vidal, "I'd like to stretch my legs for a bit, I'll walk you to your place." In a confidential tone he added, "You mustn't think my only distraction in life is sprawling in my chair watching a game on television. That's not to say, of course, that I haven't the greatest respect for the marvels technology has given us."

Why, Vidal wondered, should he find this last sentence so irritating? When they got to Vidal's house, Rey took his arm and said, "Let's walk a while longer. Come on, walk back to my place."

Vidal would have liked to be alone, to be already in bed, preferably asleep. To break the silence he remarked:

"It's not so cold tonight."

"No. It's late this year, but at last we're going to have a real Indian summer."

Vidal noted that at night it was as if there were more room, and he seemed to shake off the concerns that nagged at him during the day: his lumbago, for instance, had disappeared, or at least dwindled into a mild discomfort. When they reached the bakery he said hurriedly, "Till tomorrow."

"I'll walk you home."

It occurred to him suddenly that Rey might be wanting to say something important to him, and at the same time that if Rey could not make up his mind to speak, they might go on walking until dawn. Again he spoke in order to break the silence, "Why weren't you at the bakery yesterday?"

"Yesterday morning? Oh, is that what the girls said . . . ?"

Probably Rey was torn between needing to talk and being afraid to. But Vidal was not inquisitive, and with the selfishness of a man who is exhausted, he made up his mind to put an end to these comings and goings.

"Good night," he said, turning into his own doorway. Looking back he caught a dim glimpse of Rey's fleshy face, mouth open, just about to speak.

IX

Saturday, 28 June

The next morning his lumbago was back again. Slowly trying out several tentative movements, here and there he encountered pain. Jokingly he compared himself to a good card player, Arévalo for instance (or Jimmy doing an imitation of Arévalo), fanning out his cards with elaborate care, deliberately postponing the moment when he discovers what luck has brought him.

He presently concluded that the pain was not too severe to bear, and did not justify, for the moment, injections or any other expense at the druggist's. The next thing, he told himself, was to face bravely a genuine ordeal, the hardest of all: he had to do a light laundry. *Right this minute,* he told himself. But he pictured the effort it would take to scrub and rinse, with his back hunched forward over the tubs, and thought better of it. Mastodons they were, he thought, those old wash tubs, deep and wide. *It's a model they don't even make any more,* he protested. *It must be true, as they say, that people were taller back then.* He gathered up a pair of socks, a pair of shorts, a shirt and an undershirt. Shaking his head he thought, *There's no way out of it. Until I get my pension —and I wonder now if I ever will—I can't afford to send the laundry out. Antonia will be upset if I don't give the laundry to her mother to do. But until I get paid, this luxury is excluded, like all the rest. Here I am, talking to myself again.*

Doña Dalmacia, Antonia's mother, was the most popular tenant in the building. Widowed at an early age, this admirable woman had managed to bring up eight children, feeding and clothing them decently on nothing but what she earned by washing and ironing, joking and singing as she worked. Now, with her own children (except Antonia) married and living away from home, *doña* Dalmacia had taken in three pallid little granddaughters, since the father was having money troubles. In her generous heart there was always room for one more, and her energy was boundless. Still, age had changed her, or perhaps it was merely that her native bluntness was more apparent as the years went by—it was probably for this reason that the newcomers in the neighborhood referred to her, with affectionate mockery, as "the dragoon." But if her temper was violent—people thought twice before they made an enemy of *doña* Dalmacia—it was also true that she was quick to forgive, and bore no grudge.

On his way to the washrooms Vidal thought, *Let's hope I don't run into anybody. In this place they keep count of how many times you use the bathroom.* And of course he found Nélida doing a laundry. Faber was there with her.

"I was explaining," said Faber, "that incompetent people aren't always to blame. There are people who prod and provoke them."

"Would you believe, *don* Isidro," Nélida said, "that Antonia won't speak to me?"

"That can't be."

"Oh, no? You don't know Antonia. *Señor* Faber has done me no harm, but she's asking me to ignore him completely."

Faber nodded.

"I can't believe it," said Vidal.

"And do you know she's going around telling everybody that I was in your room the other night?"

He was unable to express the surprise that was perhaps expected of him, for at this moment Dante and Arévalo came in. (There was something odd about Dante's appearance.) Nélida left abruptly, saying, "Anyway, don't make yourselves too conspicuous."

Faber headed off quickly toward his room, and Vidal promptly ran into the custodian, who said, "We must not allow ourselves to be divided by petty disagreements. *Señor* Bogliolo, for instance, is having a fit about some water leaking in from the attic. There's no reason to make a fuss; I'm going up right now to see what the trouble is." He walked off a few yards, and then walked back. With a dramatic air he proclaimed, "Unless we present a united front, we'll be hemmed in on all sides."

He went off again, and Arévalo noted, "Everybody seems to be upset around this place, and what we need is peace and quiet. We've come to ask you something."

"I'm listening."

"There's no need to look so solemn, we'd simply like to have your opinion. Dante here decided last night . . . Shall I tell him?"

"That's what we're here for," said Dante, ill at ease. "Let's get it over with."

Arévalo said hurriedly, "He made up his mind last night to dye his hair, and he wants to know what you think of the idea."

"It strikes me as per-perfectly . . ." Vidal stammered.

"Take your time," said Arévalo.

"May I explain my misgivings?" asked Dante. "There are some people who can't stand white hair; on the other hand, there are people who are infuriated at the sight of an old man whose hair is dyed."

"And may *I* explain?" said Arévalo. "I was telling Dante how one day when I was going into an hotel with a girl we met a couple at the door. The girl I was with burst out laughing. 'Just look at that little old man,' she said. I looked. It was an old classmate of mine, younger than I was, but with his hair all white he looked like a sheep."

"Do you dye your hair?" Vidal asked him.

"Are you crazy? Thank the Lord I haven't had to yet."

"There's one objection," said Dante, who was clearly worried. "A dye job is pretty obvious."

"Not at all," replied Arévalo. "People don't really see each other. They just take in the over-all effect, and then they say that so-and-so is gray-haired or is bald."

"Women probably notice," said Vidal.

"I can't hear you," said Dante.

"They look only at other women," said Arévalo, "so they can criticize."

"People today are much more observant," Dante persisted. "I don't care what you say, the sight of an old man with dyed hair exasperates them."

"And what about the bald ones?" Vidal asked.

"Besides," Dante went on, "nowadays hair dyeing is never done right. You can always tell."

"Half the girls you see in the street have dyed hair. Can you tell which?"

"No, I can't," Dante admitted.

As though he were changing sides, Arévalo remarked, "You can tell when they use it as a disguise. For instance, what about these brunettes who bleach their hair blond?"

"I'm not concerned about the brunettes. Tell me the truth, does it make me look younger? Oh, I know nobody will be fooled by it," said Dante bleakly.

"In that case, why did you do it?" asked Arévalo.

"I don't know. I asked you for advice."

"Sometimes there's nothing to do but to take the plunge."

"That's easy to say, when it comes to other people. And you still won't tell me if it looks all right or if it looks funny. Am I even worse off than I was?"

He's nothing but a silly, peevish child, thought Vidal. Aloud he said, "What's a man to do if he's bald?"

Nélida returned. "*Don* Isidro," she said in a low voice, "Leandro is on the telephone."

"I'll be just a moment."

"No, we have to get going."

"What were you going to do with those clothes?" Nélida asked.

"Wash them."

"Give them to me."

"Antonia will be getting ideas."

"That's all we need."

To go into the shop, where half a dozen girls were working, he had to overcome a feeling of apprehension; yet the sensation of being surrounded by young women had until recently been agreeable enough.

On the telephone Rey told him, "I'm about to invest a small amount in a hotel."

"You don't mean it."

"I'd like to show it to you. Do you feel like going out this evening? It's not far from your place. Would five o'clock be too early?"

He gave him the name of the street—Lafinur—and the number.

Vidal would never have guessed that this was what had been weighing on his friend's mind the night before. He was not much of a psychologist, he thought. He never really got to know people.

X

Turning onto Lafinur Street, Vidal exclaimed, "It can't be!" But after a few steps he was forced to recognize there was no other hotel nearby. Suddenly, all of Rey's hesitation the night before became perfectly understandable: the poor man could not bring himself to say that he was thinking of buying an assignation hotel. Now it was Vidal's turn to hesitate. "It's certainly embarrassing," he said out loud, "to go in without a woman." Rey came to the door, grinning broadly and waving his hand. At what age, Vidal wondered, would he outgrow this quite irrational sense of shame and become truly mature? He had glanced around him, hoping he might perhaps go in without being observed; but now Rey, indiscreet as ever, was drawing attention to him with all his gesturing.

Rey welcomed him warmly, glad to see him, almost feverishly glad. Actually, there was no cause for the casual passerby to suppose anything out of the ordinary. Any number of reasons might bring two men such as they to meet in such a place. They might, for instance, have come with some idea of buying the place. As so often happens, the truth seemed highly unlikely.

Rey led him along a corridor opening on a patio, knocked cautiously several times at a door, opened it without waiting further, and stepped aside for Vidal to enter. Vidal hesitated a second, then walked in. He was feeling as insecure as he might have in a dream; and it cheered and steadied him to find himself face to face with a stout, sallow-complexioned man—undoubtedly the owner—seated in his office. There was a table in front of him, with cups of coffee set out.

Rey introduced them. "My friend Vidal. My buddy from the provinces, Jesús Vilaseco."

"Another cup, Paco," Vilaseco bellowed. "Strong and hot." Lowering his voice he asked, with a groan, "Can you find worse help anywhere than in a place like this? Aside from making up the beds, what is Paco good for? Nothing but bringing cold coffee and lukewarm drinks."

Paco appeared with a cup. He looked like a dolt, as whey-faced as his employer, though younger, and slovenly beyond belief.

"*Don* Jesús," he said, "the walls in number eighteen are a mess again."

"The 'Angélica' guy?"

"Not on your life. If I get my hands on that creep . . ."

"More coffee, Paco, and please, try to have it hot for once."

"Who's this Angelica fellow?" Rey asked.

"Oh, some lunatic who keeps writing on the walls, 'Angélica, I'll find you yet.' "

The poor fellow, thought Vidal. *Full of love, and empty of illusions.* "Poor man," he said aloud.

"Poor man," echoed the owner. "You'll have nuts like him to thank when they close your place down one of these days."

"What do you mean," asked Rey.

"Sooner or later he'll find the woman—and if he finds her here she won't be alone—and he'll shoot her down like a rabbit. You people on the outside think this is a real soft life."

Rey's voice was sly, "Stop complaining. Except for the undertakers, what business brings in more cash on the line than yours?"

"You're not going to compare the two? Nobody bothers them. Oh, I'll admit it takes a strong stomach, but . . ."

Here in this conversation, thought Vidal, the positions were reversed: the prospective buyer was playing up the value of the merchandise, the seller was belittling it. Had they forgotten their roles?

"And what do you know," Rey fired back, "about my struggles to meet my payments at the end of the month? Not to mention the shoplifters, and the charge customers who don't pay up."

"And have you any idea what I have to go through? You can soften up a government inspector with a slice of cake, but how can I explain the mob that flocks in here on Saturday—to say nothing of the visits I get from the Council on Public Morals and the fellows on the police force. You know the man I envy? *Don* Eladio, who went from a fleet of taxi-cabs to a chain of garages, and then into the meat-trucking business. Paco, when is that coffee coming?"

There followed a lengthy discussion of *don* Eladio. These business men, Vidal reflected, seem to be in no kind of hurry, and appear to have nothing to do at all; whereas he, unemployed, could not afford to waste his time. But perhaps if he stayed, he would be rewarded by a diverting spectacle, as these two maneuvered from their respective starting points to their respective goals, to sell high and to buy low. Nonetheless, he was growing very impatient.

Paco came and set down a pot of coffee on the table.

"If it's not hot, blame the customers. The bell hasn't stopped ringing."

"And still you complain," said Rey.

"Haven't I reason to, Leandro? All I ask is a cup of really hot coffee."

The door opened and a woman's voice asked, "May I come in?"

Paco went to see who it was.

"It's Tuna," he said. "What's new?"

"How are things?" asked the boss.

"At last you've come," said Rey, with a glance at the clock.

Tuna was short, with coppery skin, thick black hair, a narrow forehead, and prominent cheekbones; her eyes were small, with a hard look to them. Her clothes were new, but undistinguished. She had a cold.

"Coffee, Tuna?" the boss asked her. "Maybe Paco will try extra hard and serve it hot."

"Thanks, I haven't time."

"Haven't time?" asked Rey, alarmed.

"Well, yes, of course. I just meant no time to spare."

Vidal had got up from his chair. Since no one had introduced them, he nodded to her slightly.

"Well, then," the boss suggested, "if you're ready, shall we go?"

Tuna fished out a piece of kleenex from her purse, carefully unfolded it, and blew her nose vigorously. Vidal watched her hand close around the damp tissue; her nails were painted dark red. What was she doing there, he wondered, was she some sort of go-between in the transaction? It seemed unlikely.

"We'll follow you," said Rey.

Vidal was the last to leave. The rooms, with their endless row of Nile green doors, faced on a covered patio; along the right ran a closed-in driveway with a vine-covered trellis over it. The boss turned the knob of the first door.

"No, *don* Jesús, that one's occupied," Paco told him.

"The rooms look all alike," said the boss, opening the second door.

Tuna and Rey entered, the boss let Vidal in, and then withdrew, closing the door behind him. The room contained a generous-sized bed, two night tables, two armchairs, some large mirrors. "I've fallen into a trap," thought Vidal, and at once realized that this was an absurd idea. For all his weariness would he always be, deep down, a child? And what was worse, a timid child? Forever caught up in some unforeseen situation to the end of his days . . . He noticed now that Rey was fondly kissing the girl's hands.

"Either you behave yourself or I'm leaving," Tuna threatened. "I told you I had no time to waste."

"We'll be good," said Rey, resignedly.

He motioned Vidal to a chair and sat down on the edge of the bed. Sitting there like a well-mannered child, he looked very big and very fat. Absent-mindedly Vidal read the inscriptions on the walls: *Adriana and Martín, Rubén and Celia, A Lover from Entre Ríos Was Here, Pilar and Rubēn.*

Tuna had a severe head cold. She kept blowing her nose, taking the kleenex from her purse and, after using it, placing it on the empty chair.

"If you're afraid of catching more cold—" suggested Rey, full of solicitude.

"If it did me harm to take my clothes off," Tuna assured him, "I'd have tuberculosis by now."

As she removed each garment, she piled it neatly on the back of the chair. Naked, she walked around the room, and with surprising shyness, attempted a few dance steps, then raised her arms in an ecstatic pose, and did a couple of turns. From her breasts down to the pit of her stomach her skin was greyish, Vidal noted, and she had a mole near her navel. She went over to Rey, so that he might give her a kiss. Then she spoke. With a start, Vidal realized that she was speaking to him.

"You don't want to do anything either?"

"No, no thank you," he answered hurriedly. But even as he spoke he foresaw that he might later feel regret, even anger. Rey burst out laughing.

"Don't feel bashful on my account . . . Go ahead, she's all yours."

Perhaps he wanted to prove that he was master of the situation. Vidal was about to reply curtly when Tuna said, in a despondent tone, "If you don't want to do anything, at least take this for a souvenir."

She took another kleenex from her purse, pressed it against her lips, and then clumsily wrote in lipstick beneath the outline of her mouth, *From the Brunette.*

"Thank you," said Vidal.

"They call you the Brunette?" asked Rey anxiously. "You never told me you were called the Brunette."

She dressed, asked for her money, and got into a heated argument with Rey over the amount. Vidal recalled that Rey had once referred to the handing over of money as the moment of truth. But at parting, he and Tuna were the best of friends. Affectionately, like uncle and niece, they kissed each other on the cheek.

When the men were alone, Rey remarked, "She's not a bad little thing. I have others like her, a whole swarm, that I can contact by telephone . . . Did I tell you how I found her? In the classified section, under Domestic Help. The ad made such a point of her pleasing manner that it drew my attention. They're not bad girls. The only problem is that every one is linked up with a character who's—unpredictable, to say the least."

They said goodbye to the boss and went out into the street. Without knowing why, Vidal suddenly felt sorry for his friend. He wanted to say something, so that Rey should not suppose he was angry, but they walked a good distance without his finding anything to talk about. When they passed the house that was being wrecked, he commented, "Look how quickly they're razing it."

"True," Rey agreed. "In this country, the only thing we're quick about is tearing things down."

Vidal observed the demolition crew at work. What must have been a bedroom had been ripped open and exposed to the wind and rain. The wallpaper showed a discolored square where a picture must have hung, and beyond, the privacy of the bathroom was revealed. When they came to the bakery he recalled the way he had shaken off Rey the night before; and, since a single precedent is enough to establish a habit, he said abruptly, "They're expecting me. I'll leave you now."

He hurried off. When he looked back, he saw the same thing he had the night before: Rey's fleshy face, mouth still open.

XI

He was as eager to be home again as an animal to get back to its lair, but he was mildly astonished to note also that his nerves were on edge; and he decided to relax a bit before he shut himself up in his room for the night. A man his age, he thought, ought to have had enough experience not to be surprised by such incidents as that at the hotel. He compared the episode to those dreams in which there is nothing dangerous or deeply disturbing in a situation itself, but which oppress us because of the indefinable intensity of the images. There is no knowing what association of ideas led him to recall a dog his parents had had, when he was a young boy. Poor Vigilante, after years of exemplary behavior—he was the picture of unselfishness, devotion, and dignity—had taken in old age to pursuing the bitches of the neighborhood in a way that was indecorous as well as futile. For what was probably the first time in his life, Vidal had been offended. He could never have the same feeling for the dog again; and when they lost Vigilante he experienced two new emotions, remorse and grief.

It would do him good to talk to Jimmy, he thought. Jimmy, with his extraordinary good sense, would help him to see it all as a joke, to understand the meaning of this absurd trap that had been set for him. True, it would not be easy for him to tell the story without mentioning Rey's name or, more exactly, without laughing at Rey; but it was equally true that Rey had made use of him in order to achieve some mysterious purpose. In any case, he disliked the idea of behaving with conscious disloyalty toward a friend. A phrase occurred to him that might help to protect poor Rey: *Name the sin, not the sinner*. But how long would he be able to keep up the verbal fencing with Jimmy? He was not feeling too hopeful by the time he reached the house in Malabia Street, where Jimmy had been living ever since he had been paid to give up his former abode at Juncal and Bulnes. Intending to spend only a few days there, he had moved into a residential hotel but his lucky star would have it that its owner also decided to put up a new building and in order to evict the guests immediately, offered them an indemnization. Jimmy, the last arrival, demanded a larger sum than anyone else, stayed on till the last possible moment, and was now installed in an old house which still displayed, to the right of the door, a glittering sign: gold letters on a black background spelled out *New Cantabrian Hotel*. Living with him was his niece Eulalia, a matronly, faded blonde; there was much speculation about the nature of Eulalia's duties, since the bulk of the domestic tasks fell to Leticia, the day maid, a creature with a face that looked as though it had been left half-finished, and a repulsive skin, reminiscent of a mummy's.

The New Cantabrian had originally been a private home, of the kind that was built at the turn of the century, with the kitchen, larder, and pantry in the cellar. The kitchen was lighted by a semi-circular window at street level. Some movement against the background of white tiles attracted Vidal's attention.

He stopped, bent down, and looked. It seemed as though a couple was dancing in the cellar, a dance that alternated between rigid postures and sudden evasions, violent shaking and affected contortions. A moment later he realized that the woman struggling in an embrace was Leticia, and that the man pursuing her, unrecognizable in his fit of fierce urgency, was Jimmy. With their hair streaming wildly, their clothes disarranged, they looked as though they had gone berserk. Vidal, incapable of movement, stayed there, stooped over the window.

An unknown voice, very near, roused him from his stupor. "Just like a dog in heat. That filthy old man needs a lesson."

Vidal, straightening, looked up into the face of a thin young man: his attitude was condemnatory, the expression of a fanatic.

"Let's not exaggerate," Vidal said.

"Is that your opinion?" the young man asked in a tone of rejection.

Vidal managed to answer, "I shouldn't do such a thing myself, but if that's what he likes, it's his business."

More than once, on his way home, he looked behind him to make sure no one was following. This strange sequence of hotels and grotesque love scenes had ended in an ambiguous incident which left him disturbed. Had he cause for self-reproach? By his stupid curiosity he had exposed a friend, and then had not had the resolution to defend him. Condemning his cowardice, which he determined never to fall back into, he turned once more to look behind.

XII

Sunday, 29 June

"It's a beautiful morning," declared Néstor, entering Vidal's room. "Who could want to stay indoors on a day like this? How about coming to the soccer game with us?"

"I don't think so. It's still too cold."

"In here maybe. Haven't you been out yet?"

"I've been to the grocer's and the baker's. I had my mind on other things, so I was almost home before it struck me there was something strange about the city, it's the way it is on the days there's a revolution in the air. It's just not a quiet, peaceful Sunday."

"Except that you see the police posted all over. They've announced they won't tolerate any violence. Come on, let's go to the game."

"I've been thinking."

"Thinking what?"

"Foolish thoughts. That we're old. That there's no room for the old, there's no provision for them. For us, that is. Original idea, isn't it?"

"In the first place, you're not old. And besides, there's room for everyone. Life has a lot to offer . . ."

"I'm not so sure. If you walk out on Las Heras and see all the pretty girls . . . There are always plenty of them, the world is inexhaustible, each year it yields a new crop."

"It's stimulating to watch."

"You're crazy. You have to keep telling yourself they're not for you. The moment you look too closely, you become a dirty old man."

Néstor stared at him with his hen's eyes, round and expressionless, and declared, "Women aren't everything."

"How do you mean?"

"I mean that life is a long series of attractions."

"Just like a fair."

"There's a pleasure to suit every age."

Suddenly they heard a groan. Vidal hastened to reply. "Everything about old age is dismal and ridiculous, even the fear of dying."

"I suggest you to go to the soccer match. It will put you in a different mood."

"No use. When I get to Las Heras and see the women passing by . . ."

"Shall I confess something? For some time now, women have ceased to interest me."

Another groan, this time very near.

"What do you mean?"

"Just what I said. Frankly, I don't even notice them any more. And yet I can remember the time when I'd go to any length to keep a rendez-vous."

"And now they leave you indifferent?"

"Com-plate-ly."

"Com-plate-ly?" asked Vidal, mimicking.

"More or less," Néstor admitted, with a smile. "On the other hand, I've discovered the fascination of money."

Vidal looked at him with a curiosity that was not unmixed with admiration. Through all the years he had known him, he had never suspected that Néstor was capable of thinking for himself. Possibly he was not entirely mistaken in believing that life was full of surprises.

"I'm going to put on water for *maté,*" he said.

"None for me. It's getting late."

"Don't go without explaining how you came to discover the fascination of money."

"Quite by chance . . . Although these things always come about in their own good time. Chance is probably just an illusion. You know Eladio, the fellow with the garage? They were going to fine him because the bathrooms were unsanitary. It so happened the inspector was a friend of mine, and I came to the rescue. Eladio told me he'd return the favor, and that I stood to make a lot of money. I wasn't too keen, because Regina and I were quite comfortable, and we didn't need anything. But he got me started, and I put down some money on an apartment."

"So you've gone in for income property, like Rey?"

"I don't know anything about Rey's business. But for my part, in order to meet my payments I had to cut out every extra expense, including going out with Regina's friends."

"With your wife's friends?"

Still another groan.

"I ought to warn you, you have a lion in the next room."

"It's only poor Isidorito snoring."

"The first women to offer themselves to you are always your wife's friends. Human nature is a mysterious thing. On the one hand, I lost all feeling for women. Why? Simply lack of practice or, if you prefer, lack of habit. On the other hand, I found I liked being a capitalist, I wanted to increase my holdings."

"One apartment wasn't enough for you?"

"I got to thinking about how much my son would have left, once the inheritance tax was paid."

"A cheerful thought," said Vidal, mimicking Jimmy.

"On the contrary, quite natural. You're going to say anyone else would be content to live in peace, enjoying the rewards of his sacrifice. But not me; the moment I'd paid the final installment I went on to buy another apartment. That's what I'm involved in now. I've really got the fever. Seriously, why don't you come with us to watch River play?"

"Your poor son. Playing nursemaid to old men."

"When will you get it through your head that you're not old? Besides, shall I tell you something? The boy asked me specifically to invite you."

"What time are you going?"

"Twelve o'clock."

"All right. If I'm not there by twelve, don't wait for me."

"Try to be there. You could do with a change of scenery."

XIII

Isidorito was still asleep. Not so much because he was hungry but rather to allow the boy time to waken slowly, Vidal prepared a light lunch for himself: a hard-boiled egg (*In a little while it'll give me a twinge in my side,* he thought. *My newest disorder*), toast, a little cheese, a bit of quince jam, a small glass of wine. He ate hurriedly, threw his poncho over his shoulders, glanced at the clock. If he didn't waste any time, he could catch up with them.

Seeing Nélida in the hall, he recalled that she seldom got all dressed up Sundays the way Antonia and the other girls did; but today, ready to go out, she looked wonderfully pretty. He tried to find the proper way to say so to her; but his fear that it might sound like a forced and artificial compliment led him instead to speak of the weather, which was still cold.

"I don't know, it seems to me it's a little milder," said Nélida. "Indian summer."

The custodian came in, limping; he greeted them pleasantly and even joined for a moment in the conversation.

"You're right, Indian summer. But it's come late this year."

"You never can tell," said Vidal. "I'm still chilled to the bone."

As though talking to himself, the custodian went on, "Indian summer and a fine mess it is—heat and humidity, colds, grippe."

When he had left, Vidal asked, "What happened to him?"

"What do you mean?"

"He's a different person. A little bent over and limping, but the main change is that he's meek as a lamb now."

"What would you expect after the thrashing he got?"

"Ah, justice has been done, for once. He was beaten, you say?"

"Right here in the hallway. Didn't you hear the commotion?"

"Yes, now I remember. The other morning."

"Noon."

"Yes, Thursday noon." But Nélida was looking too pretty for him to go on talking about the custodian. "Where are you heading all dressed up?"

Trying to be agreeable, he had succeeded only in being clumsy and tactless.

"I'm waiting for my fiancé," Nélida replied.

The words opened a gap between them. Vidal smiled, looked at her sadly, shook his head, and departed. It was absurd enough, he thought, that he, a mature man, should get upset at the thought of courting a young girl; but it was unthinkable that it should disturb him merely to carry on a perfectly innocent conversation. Trying to recover his self-possession, he glanced around as if he were looking for something, and remarked in an undertone, "Néstor wasn't exaggerating. It's a splendid day." He walked along skirting the garbage cans which lined both sides of the street. After a friendship of so many years, why was it only now that he had come to know Néstor? Was it because he was always so detached from things? *Certainly I'm not what you'd call curious and without curiosity, they say, nothing would ever be discovered. But all the curious and inquisitive people I've known have been stupid.* Néstor had shown himself capable of seeing the truth and stating it simply. Listening to him talk about the fascination of money, as though it were a joke on himself, how was it possible not to like him? You heard lots of talk about loneliness, but with friends you were never really alone.

Beside the curb at the corner a cart was standing, with a load of empty bottles and old newspapers. On the side of the cart someone had written: "Lover available for poor girls." He was reflecting peacefully about the way popular humor makes a people aware that they form a unique entity, when he heard on the wall above him, no more than six feet to his left, a noise he understood was a crash. Before he recovered from his momentary confusion he saw the man in the cart, without any provocation whatever, take more careful aim and hurl a second bottle at him. Feeling on his face not the object itself, but the rush of air it made as it sailed past him, he looked around for help. Three or four people happened to be standing near—one had stopped just as he was about to cross the street, a couple of others were talking in the doorway of an apartment—and in that split second Vidal recognized on each face the stony-eyed expression of a hunter about to fall on his prey. Instinctively he turned around and began to run. It surprised him to find—because when he was young he had been an outstanding short-distance runner at the athletic club in Palermo—that he was tiring rapidly and making his escape at a desperately slow pace. All of this—the unprovoked attack, his fatigue (a sign of a physical decline he had not suspected), his lack of speed, almost as alarming as the attack itself—was reflected openly on his face.

Nélida, still waiting in the doorway, held out her arms to help him.

"What's happened, Isidro?"

He hesitated. Was his deep sense of demoralization justified by the act which had caused it? If he told Nélida, she would inevitably think, perhaps even say, "You're making too big an issue out of it." He would be like a child who has been frightened, and who attracts everyone's attention, until at last the truth comes out. Strange things had begun to happen to him of late. He had never been one to pick a fight, but neither had he been a coward. Now, for the second time in a week, he was going back to his room with the help of this girl. Things like this never used to happen. He would simply say nothing. What else could he do? But if Nélida questioned him too insistently, how long would he be able to keep silent? In proportion to the expectation that he would eventually arouse, the final revelation would surely be laughable, and his discredit would be even greater.

Despite all his fears, Nélida did not question him. He looked at her gratefully, understanding at the same time that if she was not curious it was probably because she was convinced there was not much to explain. Perhaps out of self-respect he blurted out, "They threw bottles at me."

Sitting beside him, on the edge of the bed, Nélida put an arm around his neck and held him close. Because she thinks of me as an old man, Vidal told himself, she coddles me as though I were a child.

XIV

Her face was very near. His eyes were fixed on her lips, the texture of her skin, her throat, her hands which seemed to him so mysterious and expressive. Suddenly he felt that not to kiss her would be an unbearable privation. *I'm insane,* he thought. He reminded himself that if he kissed her he would spoil the tenderness she had so freely and spontaneously shown. It would be a mistake which could not fail to disillusion her, revealing him as an insensitive fellow, incapable of appreciating her generous impulse, as a hypocrite whose virtue was only a mask for the grossest appetites, or as a fool rash enough to show them openly. *This never used to happen to me,* he thought, noting too that this commentary was becoming a habit with him. *In a situation like this I used to be a man face to face with a woman; but now . . .* And suppose he was mistaken, suppose in his incorrigible timidity he was missing his great opportunity? Why couldn't he look at things simply, why couldn't he understand that he and Nélida . . .

A loud voice sounded in the hallway: "Nélida! Nélida!"

The girl blushed. Vidal was on the point of suggesting that she leave by way of the next room, but fortunately checked himself: the idea was cowardly and stupid, and offensive, moreover, to her pride. Nélida smoothed her hair, her dress. Anyone seeing the two of them, Vidal reflected, would not readily accept his explanation of the facts, would call him a liar, and end most likely by calling him a fool. This thought seemed to contradict those that had crossed his mind a few seconds earlier.

With her head held high, and without a glance at him, Nélida opened the door and went out. Vidal tried to overhear. There was a silence, then a man's voice asked, "Where were you hiding yourself?"

"Don't shout," she told him.

Vidal stood up, ready to go out and defend her. Stock still, he listened, but the only sound was of footsteps moving away. Realizing that the situation was out of his hands, he stretched out again on the bed. Like a man resigned to frustrations, he pushed unpleasant thoughts out of his mind, and went to sleep. When he awoke a few minutes later, he felt cheerful and refreshed. He dismissed his concern about what might happen to Nélida: engaged couples, he realized, are forever having quarrels and forever making up. He went to the washroom, and this time he had the good fortune to meet no one. He drank from the tap and splashed cold water on his face. A pleasure. In view of the attack this morning, probably the most advisable course would be to stay shut up in his room. Hadn't he read, in some magazine or other, that a man could save himself a lot of unhappiness just by staying in his room? On the other hand, he told himself, nothing ventured, nothing gained. He resolved to go out, as he might any afternoon, to the Plaza Las Heras, and join his friends on a bench in the sunshine.

XV

HE felt cheered up when he caught sight of Jimmy. No mistaking that figure in the grey coat, worn shiny with years of ironing, seated on one of the benches near the statue of General Las Heras. The sunlight fell directly on his ruddy, pointed face, bristling with white hairs. A face like a fox's, a fox in need of a shave. And like the fox he appeared to be asleep, but yet was never taken by surprise.

"It's safer outside these days than it is at home," Jimmy said. "Have you discovered that too?"

Beneath the tone of congratulation lay a hint of malice. Vidal looked at him affectionately, knowing that these more or less insulting pleasantries were a peculiarity of Jimmy's, an expression of his outlook on life, not necessarily of how he felt about the person he was talking to. An old friendship is like a big, comfortable house where you can live as you please.

Perhaps because he had been through some bad moments—the attack on him, the hatred he had seen in the eyes of the bystanders, his headlong flight, the prolonged scene with the girl (on the whole encouraging, if it had not been ruined by an indecision which suggested he lacked courage, and by the frustration it had ended in), perhaps because all this was behind him, but even more because he felt restored now, ready to forget his failures and to face whatever might lie ahead, he felt an irrepressible sensation of well being. It had to burst out into words: like someone chanting a hymn before going into battle, he repeated to himself some lines of verse, forgotten since childhood, which his father used to recite:

> Under the bludgeonings of fate
> My head is bloody, but unbowed.

And to Jimmy he said offhandedly, "Guess what happened to me yesterday?"

Then he told him about the incident at the hotel. Jimmy was entranced. Nearly choking with laughter, the tears streaming down his congested face, he exclaimed, "How disgusting old men are. It's not enough for poor Rey to wallow in the mire, he has to have somebody watching."

"But he didn't do anything."

"That's the whole point," said Jimmy, still laughing. "He wants to humiliate himself publicly."

"How could he want to do a thing like that?"

"You don't know how shameless an impotent old man can be."

Vidal thought of Faber, lurking around the toilets and lying in wait for the girls, of Rey slobbering over Tuna's hands, of Jimmy, excited as a dog around a bitch in heat.

"They're grotesque, but they don't make me laugh," he said. "I find them offensive."

"I don't. People are getting too squeamish. I find that every old man turns into a caricature. It's enough to make you die of laughter."

"Or of grief."

"Grief? Whatever for? It couldn't be you're worried about joining the parade yourself?"

"It could be."

"Joining the procession of masks?"

"I suppose we all make up our own disguises, bit by bit."

"But the disguise never quite fits us," Jimmy replied. He was obviously stimulated by Vidal's contribution. "It's like a rented costume. A size too large. The effect is comical."

"Or frightful. Nothing but humiliation. You resign yourself quite shamelessly to being a kind of defective."

"To being really disgusting—a kind of mollusk, quivering and slimy. I'd never have expected Rey to come to that. So majestic behind his cash register, and to think of what he kept hidden from us all along, these fascinating little episodes, these cesspools . . ."

"Let's not exaggerate."

"What more do you want? He was slavering over that girl, as ravenous as when he's stuffing his mouth with the cheese and peanuts."

"Or you, when you're trying to lay Leticia," Vidal blurted out.

He was horrified by his own words. He had wanted to defend Rey, not to wound Jimmy.

Jimmy was not wounded. He responded with a burst of hearty laughter.

"You saw me from the sidewalk? I thought it was you, but I didn't have time to pay much attention. I wasn't going to let that stupid thing escape again. My guiding principle is, never pass up an opportunity. Don't you agree?

"There are opportunities and opportunities."

"Well, you wonder sometimes afterwards."

"Not so far as your charming friend is concerned."

"What's wrong with my charming friend, as you call her? Fundamentally women are all alike, and with one like that you have no worries."

"All right, but she's not very pretty, if you'll excuse my saying so."

"So I think of another woman. The main thing is for you to like some one of them. If after searching your mind you still don't find a single one that you like, you can start worrying, because that means you're getting old."

It was the same thing that always happened. You thought you had Jimmy in a corner, and the next thing you knew you were listening respectfully while he gave you advice. Jimmy was invincible.

"You're a sly one," said Vidal, with affectionate admiration. Among so many people ready to give up, Jimmy seemed like a rock, a pillar holding up the world. At least his own world, and that of his friends.

The sun had ceased to warm them, and they started for home. Jimmy turned suddenly to watch a cab driving slowly along Canning Street.

"Taking a cab?"

"Of course not. I'm observing, that's all, just observing. This is no time to doze. I'll bet you didn't notice there was a policeman riding next to the driver."

They crossed the street, passing close by the cab. An old woman sat inside it, weeping.

"What do you suppose happened?" Vidal asked.

"Best keep out of it."

"Poor woman."

"And so hideous. I won't look. It could bring me bad luck."

"I'm going," Vidal said.

"Tonight we're playing at Rey's house," Jimmy told him.

He was right, thought Vidal. *I shouldn't have looked at the old woman. I already knew life was a valley of tears.*

XVI

JUST before he got to Salguero Street, he met his son.

"What a pleasant surprise!"

"Maybe not. It seems to me you haven't quite grasped what's going on."

There was no bridging the generation gap, thought Vidal; and his next thought was, *The gap doesn't exist.* It was all the fault of that psychiatrist, that woman doctor, who was both confessor and oracle to his son. Or if not hers, then the fault of Farrell and his Young Turks. One thing was certain, he had given up hope of understanding any of the nonsense he kept hearing all the time. Changing the subject he asked, "How did the game go?"

"Don't even mention it. No team spirit at all. As Crosta was saying to me, discipline is just a myth today. The boys have only one thing on their minds, money and then more money. All week long it's liquor and women; the night before the game they stumble into the gym with their nerves all shot and then really get pooped. So when it's time for the game, they play like sleepwalkers. And people still wonder why our national sport is a shadow of what it used to be."

"I thought nobody back in those ancient days was good for anything."

"That's right. What did they know about team work and planning? You're not going to compare soccer as it used to be—when it was all up to star performers, every man for himself —with the careful planning that's required today, with every game worked out, right down to the last detail."

"Any disturbances?"

"A few, here and there in the stands, all minor. But on the whole, everything was under control—so much so that people got bored."

"Look, this is something I keep forgetting. Bogliolo asked me to sound you out."

"Sound me out?"

"About his denture. He'd like to know if there's any hope of his getting it back."

"Do you expect me to stick my neck out for him? People are out of their minds. Here I am, already in a compromising situation, and now my own father tries to push me . . ."

"What's awkward about your situation?"

"That's a beautiful question. I wasn't going to mention it, because I didn't want to worry you. But do you know what they told me?"

"No."

"The truck-driver and his gang found out somehow or other that I'd hidden you in the attic. Now they're furious."

Vidal dropped the subject: he did not want to weary his son, and above all he did not want to provoke any of those high-minded explanations that destroyed the harmony between them. As they headed toward Paunero Street he recalled the words spoken by a neighbor when Isidorito was still in the cradle: "One day you'll see them, father and son, out walking, bursting with pride in each other."

"I don't like to bother you, but you know how tiresome and overbearing Bogliolo can be."

"He'd better watch his step."

"He's not alone. He's counting on his nephew to come to the rescue."

Isidorito's face turned the color of tea with cream. With his thick lips turned down at the corners, he was the picture of absolute anxiety.

"See here," he said, "there's something you have to get through your head right now. All things considered, who, in the end, is most likely to be the victim of these pressure groups? Instead of making new difficulties for me, try for your own good to be diplomatic with both sides, and leave me in peace. I'm not in an enviable position just now."

"All right, but if the Bogliolos, uncle and nephew, descend on us . . ."

"Look, everybody's tied hand and foot. That goes for the Bogliolos too. Antonia, who used to be a fierce activist, considers herself lucky now if she escapes notice. Bogliolo's nephew will keep things quiet, if only on her account."

"What happened to Antonia?"

"Dad, wake up. You didn't even know *doña* Dalmacia had a stroke?"

"Poor woman."

"Poor nieces, you mean. The disease starts inside and works its way out. It's destroyed some control center or other in the brain; the result is that she's lost all restraint, and has really turned into a man. If someone doesn't get her nieces away from her, they'll be beaten to a pulp. It's terrible!"

That's no way to speak of a woman who might be your grandmother."

"In the first place, who said I wanted a grandmother? Besides, the woman has become just an animal asking to be exterminated. What more do you want anyway? So long as they're busy mending their own fences, there's a good chance they'll leave you alone."

Turning the corner at Paunero Street, he sensed abruptly, and with absolute certainty, that he was alone. He looked at the place where Isidorito was supposed to be, and found no one. He turned around. Isidorito was walking away toward Bulnes.

"Aren't you coming home?" Vidal shouted.

"Of course, I'll be there. I've got something to do. I'll be along after." He sounded querulous.

Probably, Vidal thought, *in every life a time comes when, whatever you do, you only bore people. Only one way remains of regaining your prestige, and that way is dying.* He added, a trifle ambiguously, *When there's so little time left, it seems hardly worth the trouble.*

He had reached home. His fear that Bogliolo, stationed in the doorway, might have overheard him talking to himself, led him to greet the man effusively.

"How are you, *señor* Bogliolo? What's new?"

For a moment Bogliolo made no reply. Finally he answered, "Don't be surprised if I don't return your greeting. If a man doesn't do me a service I've asked of him, so far as I'm concerned he's dead. I'll go even further: I attach no more importance to him than I should to a scrap of garbage."

Vidal looked up at him, hunched up his shoulders, slunk off to his room. With the door closed behind him, he promised himself that if he ever turned into a giant he would thrash Bogliolo to a pulp. His room was cold. *How strange,* he thought. *I was talking about the fellow to Isidorito, and a few minutes later I run into him.* Such portents, he thought—though they may be mere coincidences—remind us that life, so concrete and limited to someone searching for evidence of a life beyond, is forever involving us in nightmares which are disagreeably supernatural. He put water on to boil. He must remember to discuss these portents with Arévalo. In their youth they had had great philosophical discussions in the course of their interminable nightly walks; later on, apparently, life had wearied them. He carried in the tea kettle and the *maté* and settled down in his rocking chair. He poured and drank, occasionally rocking back and forth. He closed his eyes. From the street came the sound of an old-time automobile horn. When he heard the streetcar in the distance, coming out of a curve, then starting up with a metallic screech before putting on speed again, he realized that he was dreaming. If he recalled nothing of what had happened afterward, then a hope remained that it was dawn, that he was back in the house on Paraguay Street, with his parents asleep in the next room. He heard a dog barking. That would be Vigilante, he thought, chained to the wisteria tree. He imagined or dreamed of a conversation with his son in which he was telling Isidorito about his dream, and Isidorito thought it was comical: those old streetcars, and those automobiles whose horns made such ridiculous noises. It was hard, in retrospect, to tell what he had thought and what he had dreamed. He believed he understood, for the first time, why people say life is a dream: if you live long enough, the events of a lifetime, like the events of a dream, cannot be communicated, simply because they are of no interest to anyone. Human beings themselves, after death, become figures in a dream to the survivors, they fade away and are forgotten, like dreams that were once convincing, but which no one cares to hear about. There are parents who find in their children a receptive audience, with the result that in the child's credulous imagination they find a last semblance of life, which quickly dims out as if they had never existed. He was lucky, he told himself, in still having his friends: Néstor, Jimmy, Arévalo, Rey, Dante. Actually, he must have been dreaming, for it startled him when there was a knock on his door. The room was in total darkness. Vidal ran a hand through his hair, straightened his tie, opened the door. He could barely make out the figures of two men.

XVII

After a moment's hesitation he recognized Eladio, the garage owner. The other man, who stayed in the background, was someone he did not know.

Obeying some ancient tradition of hospitality, Vidal said, "What is it gentlemen, can I help you? Come in, please, come in."

Eladio was middle-aged and rather short: he was close-shaven, his nose was off-center, his lips expressed disapproval. He pronounced "s" like "sh," as though his mouth might be full of saliva.

"No, thanks. We have to get back to our friends."

"Don't stand in the doorway. Come in, please."

But they would not come in, and it did not occur to Vidal to turn on the light. He sensed in Eladio's attitude a certain reticence which irritated him. What was the other man doing there, who was he, and why did Eladio not introduce them? The fellow stayed back in the darkness of the hall. *Either I know him, or I've seen him somewhere recently,* Vidal thought. Eladio was obviously nervous. Having come and disturbed him, it seemed to Vidal that the least they could do was to explain at the outset what they were there for. They had aroused him from his sleep or his reverie, and now their behavior was incomprehensible. He was about to ask them once more to step inside when he saw that Eladio was smiling timidly. The smile was so unexpected that it left Vidal speechless. And no less surprising than the smile itself were the words that followed.

"Something very unfortunate has happened. I don't know how to tell you." He smiled meekly and repeated, "I don't know how to tell you. That's why I brought this boy along, for support, you might say, because I'm no good at this sort of thing, and I didn't want to come by myself. I'm so confused I haven't even introduced Paco. You know Paco, the boy who works at the hotel? I hate to think of how poor Vilaseco will manage to attend to his customers, with nobody to help him. I can see him now running from one bed to another . . ."

"Look, even if it's bad news, tell me what's happened."

"Néstor's been killed."

"No!"

"It's the truth. In the grandstand. I know it's hard to believe."

"Where is the wake?" Vidal asked, recalling how Jimmy had made fun of him when he had asked the same question a few days earlier.

"I don't know where it will be, but his friends are at the house, with the widow."

"How is his son?"

"Don't ask me questions I can't answer. I suppose he's involved in the usual formalities, because it was a case of death by violence. I'd like to say, *don* Isidro, how sorry I am. I know you were great friends. I was very fond of Néstor myself. Well, we must go now."

"I'll go with you. Will you wait for me? Just let me get my poncho. I don't know, it seems to me it's turned cold again."

He was turning the key in the lock when he heard the sound of laughter in the hall. It was Nélida, Antonia, and Bogliolo. Abruptly they all fell silent. As he passed them he nodded his head slightly. The girls, and even Bogliolo, he thought, would surely understand and respect his grief. And the respect which he attributed to them filled him with a sensation that was akin to pride. In the street a disturbing question came to his mind:

what was Nélida doing with Bogliolo? His friend was dead, he thought, and already he was beginning to forget him. Actually, this reproach was unjust because Néstor's death was affecting him at that moment, the way a fever might, dividing his consciousness, changing the aspect of everything to the point that the yellowish walls looming up on either side seemed to be closing in on him like the walls of a prison. Far off he caught sight of three or four bonfires in a row, with their red glare and flickering shadows giving the street a deeper perspective. This spectacle was oppressive too.

As though explaining, Eladio said, "It's the feast of St. Peter and St. Paul, when the children and the young people frolic around the bonfires."

"Such energy," said Vidal. "They look like demons."

XVIII

Néstor's friends were gathered in the dining-room around a kerosene stove, talking animatedly and smoking. On top of the stove was a saucepan of water and eucalyptus leaves. The wall-clock was still stopped at twelve. Jimmy was reading out loud from a newspaper. All of them stopped talking to greet the new-comers. Somebody shook his head and Rey asked Vidal in a melancholy tone, "Terrible, isn't it?"

Vidal noticed that Arévalo was wearing a new suit. He thought, *No dandruff. Well-groomed. I must talk to Jimmy about this. There's some mystery here.* He remembered Néstor, and asked, "How did it happen?"

"We haven't all the data we require in order to judge," replied Rey pompously.

"That good-for-nothing son of his should never have gone along with it," said Jimmy.

"What are people saying?" Dante asked.

"You can all testify that I did everything in my power to disuade him," said Rey. "I told him it was suicide."

"The poor fellow thought that if he went with his son nothing would happen to him," said Arévalo.

"I told him it was suicide," said Rey again.

"Poor boy," said Vidal. "What a weight on his conscience."

"I doubt it will keep him awake nights," said Jimmy.

"Who are you talking about?" asked Dante.

Rey answered, "I said it was suicide."

A stout, placid gentleman came in. He had enormous hands that looked gleaming wet, though clearly they were dry, and his voice was faint and soft. Someone explained that he was related to Néstor or to *doña* Regina.

"Where is *doña* Regina?" Vidal asked.

"In her quarters," answered Rey majestically.

"May I see her?"

"The woman from next door is keeping her company," Dante told him.

"May I see her?" he asked again.

"Don't bother her," said Jimmy impatiently. "After all, you've never even laid eyes on her."

"What were you reading when I came in?" Vidal asked Jimmy.

Two boys came in. One was square in the middle of adolescence—skinny, his face a mass of pimples. The other was short, with a round face, and bulgling eyes that gazed upward with ill-concealed curiosity. With a nervous nod of the head to the other guests, they sat down at the other end of the room. *The end where it's coldest,* thought Vidal. *The oldsters had the luck to get possession of the stove. The combined odors of eucalyptus and kerosene is the smell of the grippe.* He thought of Néstor again.

"See them?" asked Jimmy, indicating the two youths. "I don't like the looks of that pair."

"What were you reading?"

"A column in the paper about 'The War on the Pig.'"

"The war on the pig?" repeated Vidal.

"I wonder," said Arévalo, "why they say 'on the pig.'"

"'On' sounds wrong to me," said Rey.

"No, not that," protested Arévalo. "My question is why they say *pig*. This country is never consistent about anything, not even in the use of words. We always said *hog*."

"The whim of one journalist is enough," said Rey, "to start

the whole country talking about the war *on* the pig."

"You're mistaken," Dante told him. "*Crítica* calls it 'The Owl Hunt.' "

"I like the sound of that better," said Arévalo. "The owl is the symbol of philosophy."

"But admit," Jimmy said, pointing to him and Rey, "that you both prefer to be called *hogs*."

They all laughed. The woman from next door came in carrying cups of coffee on a tray.

"Gentlemen, remember your manners. There's a death in the house."

"Have they brought him home yet?" Vidal asked.

"Not yet, but it's still a house of mourning," the woman answered. "Will you have some coffee?"

"How awful," said Dante. "They've brought him home, and we carry on as though nothing had happened."

Stirring his coffee, Vidal asked Jimmy, "Tell me, why did they choose owls and pigs?"

"Beats me."

"Where did they get the idea? They say," explained Arévalo, "that old people are greedy, selfish, materialistic, and eternally grumbling. Real hogs."

"They have a point," said Jimmy.

"We'll see how you feel when they nab you," said Dante.

"What are you talking about?" retorted Jimmy. "Everybody tells me I'm in my prime."

"That's what they tell me too," Rey assured him.

"I'm tired of hearing it," said Dante.

"It's not the same thing," said Jimmy irritably.

"The Eskimo and the Lapps take their aged away, and leave them to die of cold," said Arévalo, "and you can't say they've no grounds. The only arguments in defense of the old are purely sentimental: think of all they've done for us, they have feelings too, they suffer, and so forth."

Jimmy was feeling jovial again. "Luckily for us the young

don't realize that, otherwise we'd be in a bad way. I doubt that even the activists in the Youth Committees . . ."

"What's serious," said the man with the enormous hands, "is that they don't need good reasons. Just the ones they happen to have are enough."

A thin, sharp-faced man came in. "Do you know how it happened?" he asked.

"If you ask my opinion," said Arévalo, "there's nothing behind this war on the aged except sentimental arguments in favor of youth."

"Do you know how it happened?" the newcomer asked again. "Apparently he was thrown to the ground and trampled on by people going up and down the stands."

"Poor Néstor," cried Vidal, "trampled on by those animals."

From the other end of the room the tall young man announced, "Here they come."

"Well, I must get back to my business," said Eladio. "Whether we're here or not can't make any difference to poor Néstor."

"You owe me some money," Rey told his friends. "I ordered a wreath, from all of us."

"Either it's solid gold or they robbed you," said Dante, paying his share.

"Didn't I tell you, Isidro," said Jimmy, with a wink, "that wreaths are expensive?"

XIX

In spite of their long years of friendship, it was the first time he had been in Néstor's room. Glancing vaguely at the pictures of people who were unknown to him, he thought, *The private life that each of us kept to himself didn't stand in the way of our friendship.* The idea suggested an aphorism: *People nowadays are intimate with everyone and friends of no one.*

"The poor man is all disfigured," a woman said.

The news of Néstor's death had not affected him so much as hearing these words now. Poor man. *I'm crying like a baby,* he thought. *Or like a drunken fool. I'm ashamed of myself.*

He closed his eyes. He did not want his last memory of Néstor to be his death mask. He was getting ready to say something to *doña* Regina, but she seemed so old, so crushed and broken, that he drew back the hand that he had already extended. He went back to the dining-room.

"Did you know," Arévalo asked him, "that tall skinny kid was in the stands?"

Vidal went over to the youth with the pimples. "Did you see him killed?"

"I didn't actually see it. But after talking to more than one eye-witness, I can pretty well reconstruct what happened."

Vidal eyed him with distaste. "Is it true he was trampled on?"

"How could he have been trampled on, if he was at the top of the stands? . . . You want to know how it happened? The game was late starting, the crowd was bored, and somebody suggested, 'Why don't we throw an old man over the edge?' And the second old man they threw over was *señor* Néstor."

"His son didn't defend him?"

"If I understand properly," said the man with the enormous hands, "there are people who state that he did not. Am I right?"

"Right," the boy told him. Then he added coldly, "Who doesn't have some old person in his family? There's nothing wrong in that. There are some of them that defend their old folks."

Vidal realized that Jimmy was nudging him. The sharp-featured man asked, "You're positive he was not trampled on?"

"Why should he be trampled on," the young man retorted. "He fell from the top of the stands and was crushed like a toad."

"Jimmy," said Vidal, "let's go over and talk to Rey. What do you think of those two kids?"

"You can have them."

Vidal stretched out his hands to the fire. "Why does somebody who feels like that come to the wake?"

"You mean the boys?" Rey asked. "He and the other fish-faced one are here because they belong to the fifth column."

As though he were suddenly waking up and hearing what was going on, Dante prophesied, "The facts will bear me out. You'd better believe it, we're in a real rat trap. If those two give the slightest sign, their confederates out in the street will be in here."

"More coffee?" asked the woman from next door.

"Where is Néstor's son?" Vidal asked her.

"Traitors stay out of sight."

"You won't be able to pay your respects," said Jimmy ironically.

"People say that these days you're safer out than you are at home," Rey said.

"Yes, because being at home, don't you see, means being in the trap," Dante repeated.

Rey explained to them. "The government, to keep up appearances, is no longer tolerating any outbreak in public places."

"I wonder if poor Néstor would agree," said Jimmy.

"An isolated case," Rey argued.

Once again Dante compared houses to rat traps. Arévalo joined the four of them, along with the man with the enormous hands and the one with the pointed face. Vidal noted that the two young men were again by themselves.

"The government has at last stepped in," stated the man with the large hands. "I find the minister's pronouncements reassuring. There's something noble and dignified about them."

"Very dignified," Arévalo agreed, "but they're scared out of their wits."

"To tell the truth, I don't envy the government," admitted the man with the enormous hands. "You have to realize they're in a very difficult position. Without the support of the young officers and the conscripts, the government would fall, and we'd have anarchy. An isolated case here and there is simply the price we have to pay."

"What got this started?" asked Arévalo. "What's all this talk about isolated cases?"

Jimmy explained to him, "They listened to the minister's communiqué last night. He stated that the situation was perfectly under control, except for a few isolated cases."

"What can you expect?" asked the man with the big hands. "Speaking for myself, I sense a note of new dignity and firmness, a new assurance."

The wreath arrived from the florist's.

"What did you order inscribed on the ribbon?" asked Dante.

" 'The boys,' " answered Rey. "It seemed to me those two words said it all."

"Won't it sound like it's from the young people?" Jimmy asked.

"That would be the last straw," said Rey. "You mean to say we're not the boys anymore?"

The man with the sharp face commented, "Some of the old people practice no restraints whatever. It almost amounts to a provocation."

"The ones who are provoking all this," declared Dante, "are the agents in the pay of the Young Turks."

"You think so?" asked the man with the sharp nose. "Do you suppose that old man in Caballito was hired too, the one who took liberties with those school girls?"

The man with the enormous hands declared, "It must be admitted that senile delinquency is on the increase. You read about it every day."

"Lies meant to stir up people," Dante protested.

"You have to watch out what you say," Jimmy whispered to Vidal. "Do you know the man with the big hands? I don't know either one of them. They could very well be hired informers, conspiring with the young ones. Come on, let's get out of here."

"When I think," said Vidal, "that I might have gone to the match along with Néstor."

"You had a narrow escape," Jimmy told him.

"Perhaps between the two of us we could have defended ourselves, and Néstor would be alive right now."

"Or perhaps we'd have a double wake on our hands."

"I didn't know soccer interested you particularly," said Arévalo.

"It doesn't," said Vidal, suddenly feeling important, "but since Néstor's son had specially invited me . . ."

"He had specially invited you?" echoed Arévalo.

Jimmy let out a whistle.

"What's wrong?"

"Nothing."

"You don't think they've got me tagged as an old man."

"Nonsense," said Arévalo.

"That's what I'd say myself, but with these kids today you can never be sure. If they call a man old at sixty . . ."

"The girls are the worst," said Jimmy, already amused. "They'll talk to you about their fiancés and tell you, 'He's not young, he's past thirty.' "

"This is no joke. Tell me the truth, do you think they've got me singled out?"

"What a crazy idea."

"But if I were you, I'd keep my eyes open," Jimmy advised him.

"Naturally," said Arévalo. "That's just commonsense."

Vidal stared at him incredulously.

"No reason to be caught napping," said Jimmy.

"I have a headache," muttered Vidal. "Anyone got an aspirin?"

"There must be some in Néstor's room," said Rey, getting up.

"No, don't." Jimmy stopped him. "It could bring bad luck. Have you been watching those two kids? They're peering outside every other minute."

"They look nervous," said Dante.

"Bored, that's all," said Arévalo.

I'm the one who's nervous, Vidal said to himself. His head ached, and the odors of kerosene mixed with eucalyptus were making him ill. *My feet are frozen.* On the pretext of warding off bad luck, Jimmy was depriving him of aspirin. Plainly, Jimmy's head did not ache. Vidal longed to be by himself, to breathe the night air, to walk a few blocks. *Just so long as they don't ask me where I'm going. So long as they don't come with me.* The man with the large hands and the one with the sharp nose (somebody had said one or the other of them was named Cuenca) were coming over again. Vidal stood up . . . His friends asked no questions when they saw him go; probably they supposed the presence of the two strangers accounted for his departure.

The street was enveloped in darkness. *Darker than it was a while back. Somebody's been having fun smashing the street lamps. Or else they're setting up an ambush.* Glancing distrustfully at the rows of trees, he noted that no one could be concealed behind the first few, but beyond the third or fourth the night was impenetrable. Going forward would mean exposing himself to an attack which, even though he was forewarned, could come suddenly. He was tempted to turn back, but he felt too discouraged, he hadn't the heart. He thought of Néstor. *We go through life unheeding,* he thought, *in a state of distraction.* If he reacted, roused himself from that state of unawareness, it would be to think of Néstor, of death, of people and things which had gone, of himself, of old age. *A great grief sets you free,* he thought. Indifferent to everything, he began to walk down the middle of the street, because in any case he did not wish to be taken by surprise. He suddenly glimpsed, a little ahead, a dim shape, its outlines more intensely black than the darkness of the night. *A tank,* he thought. *No, it must be a truck.* A light blazed up, very near. Vidal did not turn away, perhaps he did not even close his eyes; he held his head up, kept his face expressionless. Blinded by this flood of light, he felt an astonishing exhilaration; the thought of dying in this radiance exalted him like the prospect of victory. For a few seconds he stood there, totally absorbed by this dazzling whiteness, incapable of thought or memory. Then the headlights backed away, the beams picked out tree-trunks, the fronts of houses. He saw the truck drive off with its crowd of silent passengers; the sides of the truck were red, with white designs. Not without pride he thought, *If I'd run for it like a scared rabbit, they'd have cut me down. They probably didn't expect me to face up to them.* The night air and a kind of inner satisfaction had relieved his tension: the headache no longer oppressed him. He found himself suddenly using military terms: *With the enemy repelled, I am master of the field.* Slightly abashed, he tried to put it more modestly: *I didn't give ground. They've gone now. I'm alone.* Though he might go back inside now, he would never again reveal any haste (to anyone else, or even to himself) in running to find cover. As if he had acquired a taste for courage, he advanced down the dark street, resolved not to return until he had walked three blocks. But his display of valor was rather pointless, he thought, since at the moment he went back into the house, he would inevitably get the feeling that he was taking shelter.

XX

When he saw that Jimmy was not in the dining-room, his first thought was that he must be in the bathroom; he would go himself, the moment Jimmy came out. Clearly, he had been a little nervous, and it had been cold outside. People were still split up into two groups: the elders at the left, huddled around the stove, and the young ones at the right. His little walk must have put new spirit into him: he heard himself saying aloud, to anyone who might care to listen, "The thing that infuriates me about this war on the pig" (he was annoyed with himself for having involuntarily used this phrase to refer to the persecution of the aged) "is the deification of youth. They're acting insanely, just because they're young. That's stupid."

"Youth is a short-term condition," admitted the pop-eyed young man.

Perhaps because he had not expected anyone to agree with him so promptly, Vidal uttered something imprudent: "Of course there are valid arguments against old people."

Fearful of being questioned—he was not sure he remembered these arguments, and he had no desire to furnish arms to the enemy—he tried to go on, but the short young man interrupted. "I know, I know very well."

"You may, perhaps, but what about those overwrought kids, the real delinquents, what do they know? Arturo Farrell himself . . ."

"An agitator, I'll grant, and a phoney."

"The sad part of it is, there's nothing else behind the movement. Absolutely nothing. It's awful."

"Oh no, sir. That's where you're wrong."

"You think so?" Vidal asked, and perhaps in search of support, he glanced toward Arévalo.

"I'm positive. There are serious people behind it—people in such fields as medicine, sociology, planning. Very confidentially, there are churchmen behind it too."

You've got the face of a fish, Vidal thought. Aloud he said, "And all these enlightened minds have found no better arguments?"

"Please! The reasoning may be faulty, but it's perfectly calculated to inflame the masses. What the leaders want is swift, decisive action. Believe me, the Central Committee is guided by different motives. Altogether different, I assure you."

"You're quite sure?" asked Vidal, glancing again toward Arévalo.

"Of course," said the young man with the pimples. "That's why they liquidated the governor—you remember the case—who refused to have a motto removed from the state flag. 'To govern is to populate,' I think was the way it ran. And there was some other equally irresponsible slogan, but I forget now how it goes."

"In my opinion," said the short young man, "the chief fault lies with the doctors. They've filled up the world with old people, without prolonging human life by a single day."

"What do you mean?" asked the pimply young man.

"Do you know many people a hundred and twenty years old? I don't."

"You're right: all they've done is to people the planet with old folks who are just about useless."

Vidal thought of Antonia's mother.

"The old man is the first victim of the population explosion," the short young man declared. "To me the second victim seems much more important. I mean the individual. You'll see. Individuality will become a luxury denied to rich and poor alike."

"Isn't all this a trifle premature?" Vidal asked. "Like curing a patient who's perfectly well?"

"You've just put it in a nutshell," said the boy with the pimples. "Preventive medicine."

"While we sit here theorizing," said Vidal, "people are being murdered. We've only to think of poor Néstor."

"Horrible, but that's the way it's always been. If I had any say in the matter, I'd leave the old people in peace—they know what the world is like, after all—and organize a second slaughter of the innocents."

"Think of all the dreary protests you'd hear then," said the boy with the pimples. "You're pouring out the life-blood of the nation, the child is the future of the country. Can't you just hear the mothers shrieking?"

"I'm not worrying about them. They'd know better than to attract attention."

For the second time that night Vidal reflected that we go through life like sleepwalkers. While he had been absorbed in his own trivial concerns (above all with following a rigid routine: his *maté* at a certain hour, his siesta, his hurry to reach the Plaza Las Heras to enjoy the afternoon sun, the games of *truco* at the cafe), great changes had taken place in the country. These young people—the one with the pimples and the shorter one who seemed to be intelligent—spoke of these changes as something known and familiar. Probably because he had not followed the process, he did not understand the world around him. *I've been left behind,* he thought. *And now I'm old, or getting ready to be.*

XXI

"What are you thinking about, sir?" asked the short young man, not unpleasantly.

"I'm thinking that I'm old," he replied, immediately wondering if he was not overstepping the bounds of prudence. He might end by getting himself into trouble.

"Pardon me," the young man protested. "In my opinion that's sheer nonsense. You're not old. I'd place you in the zone which that fraud Farrell calls 'no man's land.' You couldn't be called young, but you're certainly not old either."

"The thing is," Vidal said, "that one of these young lunatics on the loose might make a mistake."

"A mistake of that kind is unlikely, but I can't deny it's a possibility," the young man admitted, adding hastily, "in view of all the current unrest."

Again Vidal felt depressed: why had he not clung to his blissful ignorance? Talking to these boys appeared like a miserable attempt to get into their good graces. "Excuse me," he muttered. So as to be more at ease, he went back to his friends.

Rey was declaiming, "We shall see what the government does when the hour of truth arrives. When it pays what it owes us."

"You'd better realize that hour is due to be postponed," Arévalo told him. "Even if they succeed in restoring order, they're not going to pay us."

"Where's Jimmy?" asked Vidal.

"Don't interrupt," said Dante, who had probably not understood. "We're talking about serious matters. About our pension."

"The government won't make any move to pay it," insisted Arévalo.

"You have to admit," said the man with the large hands, "that it would require a great deal of courage to issue an order for payment. It would be an unpopular measure, and would naturally arouse strong opposition."

"And fulfilling commitments counts for nothing?" Rey inquired.

"I've heard talk these last few days," said the sharp-featured man, "of some plan to compensate the aged by offering them land-grants in the south."

"Why not speak plainly and call it mass deportation?" Dante asked.

"Like cannon fodder," said Rey.

"And it would put a stop to the trouble they're having with Chileans slipping across the border," said Arévalo.

"Where's Jimmy?" Vidal asked.

"What?" asked Arévalo. "He went looking for you. Didn't you see him?"

"Could he have gone to the bathroom?"

"I saw him go out that door," said Rey. "He can't stand get-togethers like this, and he grabs the first chance to sneak away to his den."

"He told us he was going to look for you," said Rey again.

"I didn't see him."

"A real fox," Dante persisted. "He's gone home, back to his lair. We know him pretty well."

"We knew poor Néstor too, his whole life," Arévalo replied. "I'm going to see if Jimmy's home."

"I'll go with you," said Rey.

"Anybody would think condolences were already in order," said the sharp-faced man with a laugh. "I wouldn't worry, if I were you; he'll be back any minute."

"I'm going," said Vidal. "He went out to find me, it's my place to go."

"All right," said Arévalo, "we'll go together."

Arévalo put on his raincoat, Vidal threw on his poncho. They paused for a moment in the doorway, peered into the darkness, and went out.

"It's not a question of being afraid," Vidal remarked. "It's just that one dislikes the idea of being surprised."

"Above all if that's what you're expecting. Anyway, if I'm going to die, I don't care to leave the initiative to these idiots. On the other hand, illness doesn't tempt me either. And if you shoot yourself, or jump from a window, you're bound to get a disagreeable shock. And if you swallow an overdose of pills and then change your mind, what happens then?"

"You might as well stop there because you're going to end up preferring the idiots. But the two who were there tonight told me our names were not on the list."

"Then they're not such idiots after all. They've found out no old man admits to being old. And you believed them? They're putting our minds at rest just to make their own job easier."

"You think it's wrong to expose myself like this?"

"I don't understand."

"These trees stand out so, even in the darkness. A fine figure I'd cut if they attacked right now."

He was urinating against a tree. Arévalo followed suit.

"It's the cold. Cold and old age. A need that's become one of the most constant occupations of our life."

They resumed their walk in slightly better spirits.

"One of those boys was explaining to me . . ." Vidal began.

"The one with the face of a fish?"

"It doesn't matter, they're two of a kind."

"He was explaining that there were valid reasons for this war on the pig."

"And you believed him? People don't kill for valid reasons."

"He talked about the growth of the population, and how the number of useless old people is constantly increasing."

"People kill out of stupidity or fear."

"Still this problem of useless old people is not just something they've dreamed up. Remember Antonia's mother, the one they call the dragoon?"

Arévalo was not listening. He said flatly, "In this war, what drives the youngsters to kill is their hatred of the old people they will become themselves. A hatred that's mostly fear."

It was cold, they hastened their steps. As if by some unspoken agreement they skirted entire blocks to avoid the bonfires, going hundreds of yards out of their way, and came to a section where the street lights had not been smashed.

"With things lit up," said Vidal, "you can hardly believe there's a war going on."

They arrived at Jimmy's house. "Everybody's asleep here," said Arévalo.

They looked in vain for a crack of light between the blinds.

"Shall we ring?" Vidal asked.

"Let's."

Vidal pushed the button; they could hear the bell ringing in the back of the house. After a couple of minutes, he asked, "What shall we do?"

"Ring again."

He pressed the button once more, and again they heard the jangle of the bell.

"And suppose Dante was right, and Jimmy's already asleep?" Vidal asked.

"Too bad. We'll look like the alarmists we are."

"Yes, but if something's happened to him . . ."

"Nothing's happened. He's a sly old fox."

"You think so?"

"Sure. Let's go, we don't want to be taken for a couple of old-maid aunts."

A bonfire was burning in the distance. Vidal was reminded of a picture he had seen as a child: Orpheus, or some devil perhaps, wrapped in hell-fire, playing the violin.

"How stupid," he said.

"What?"

"Nothing. The bonfires. The whole business."

XXII

RETURNING to Néstor's house, they found their friends preoccupied.

"Something's happened," Arévalo whispered.

"That's what's happened," Vidal told him, and he pointed to Bogliolo's nephew.

Whenever someone new comes in, he thought, *the grief is renewed. I've watched it happen. The ones already here have accepted the law of nature: life must go on, the best you can do is to think of something else, get your mind off it. But each newcomer makes the cadaver evident again.*

Dante's voice startled him out of his reverie. "They say Jimmy has been kidnapped."

"Who says so?" asked Arévalo.

"It's rumor that's circulating among the young people," said Bogliolo's nephew.

Rey uttered a hoarse cry, his swollen face turned purple, he panted for breath. *When he's angry, this man must be like some wild animal, like an enraged bull,* said Vidal to himself, but his mind turned back at once to Jimmy. He and Arévalo should not have been so hesitant, they should never have come back without being certain that Jimmy was really at home.

"We didn't try long enough, you know. We rang the bell only twice."

"If you'd kept it up," said Dante, "and made sure Jimmy

wasn't there you wouldn't have accomplished much except to get the women all upset."

"We were simply trying to find out what had happened," said Vidal.

"The poor devil said he was going to look for you," explained Rey. "He went out that door. It was the last we saw of him."

Vidal led Bogliolo's nephew to the other end of the room and said firmly, "This concerns only the two of us. If it's true they've nabbed Jimmy, try to find them, and, please, ask them to release him. When they balk, tell them I'll take charge of dealing with them."

"How am I going to contact them?" answered the young man in a whining tone.

I wonder if I let myself get carried away, thought Vidal. *I had to do something for Jimmy. The other day I stood gaping like an idiot at his window and exposed him to all this. Tonight I stroll out, just to prove how brave I am, and he gets kidnapped.*

He went back to his friends. Rey, in a towering rage, was muttering something or other about Néstor's son and Bogliolo's nephew.

"What is it?" asked Dante, with a smile. "What were you saying?"

"Frankly it sounds suspicious to me," Arévalo agreed. "The youth clubs were awfully quick to pass out the word."

Vidal thought of how proud Néstor had been of his son. And then he thought of his own son: had Isidorito heard of the latest developments, and did he have the courage to condemn them?

"This passivity is unworthy of us," said Rey. "If I have to die, at least it would be a comfort to make mincemeat of a few of these brats. Why don't we tell that one over there that somebody's asking for him, and load him off to the kitchen?"

"And once you've got him there?" asked the man with the enormous hands.

"Why I'd throttle him, that's all."

"But that would be a criminal act, wouldn't it?" asked the sharp-featured man.

"It's as though there were some unspoken agreement," remarked Arévalo, "that one half of society may exceed the bounds and the other may not. That's the way it's always been."

"I don't buy that," Rey declared. "And since, thank God, I've got the will and the strength for it, I'm going to indulge myself and teach one of those kids a lesson . . . but no—" he exclaimed, "our bird has just flown the coop."

They turned to the door in time to see Bogliolo's nephew wave goodnight and leave. Vidal wondered if he should feel thankful. Once again the woman from next door appeared with another round of coffee.

"*Señora,*" Dante asked her, "could you explain what reason you had for saying it was Néstor's own son who gave him away."

"Don't put words into my mouth," the woman protested. "I'm accusing no one, and I don't like to be accused myself."

Arévalo was cleaning his glasses. In his asthmatic voice he said, "She has every reason to be wary. One of these young punks has probably threatened to slit her throat if she opens her mouth again."

"They threaten and they kill," said Rey, "and we sit here with our arms folded."

Vidal heard the throb of an engine and the screech of brakes.

"And there's another possibility," said Arévalo. "Maybe the shrewd old lady has sniffed something in the air—like a change for the worse."

"Isn't it more likely the woman got flustered when you asked her a direct question?" said the man with the enormous hands. "The way students do in an examination?"

"Careful," whispered the sharp-featured man. "Don't look around. Just go on talking, as though nothing had happened."

Vidal glanced around: four young men had burst into the room. Not only did he glance at them, but, perhaps because he did not immediately grasp what was going on, he looked straight into the eyes of the one who appeared to be the leader. For a few seconds the two confronted each other in silence; then the chief marched over to the two young men, and the other three followed. The tramp of their heavy boots echoed through the house; until this moment everyone had been walking on tiptoe and speaking in whispers. Suddenly the wall-clock started ticking again.

The man with the enormous hands sounded as though he had only a thread of voice left. "There's no mistake what they are."

"What are they?" asked Dante.

"Hoodlums who have no respect for a house in mourning."

"Hoodlums and boors," echoed the man with the sharp features, in a voice that had sunk to a mere whisper.

The new arrivals and the two young men were having a lively discussion. Now and then they would glance briefly at the older men or, without looking, point a finger in their direction. The tick of the clock heightened the tension in the air.

"It's only four or five steps from here to the door," said the sharp-faced man.

"Once we're outside we'll be safe," said the man with the enormous hands.

"Stay where you are, or I'll drop you in your tracks," Rey ordered.

Vidal looked on, like some detached observer viewing the scene from a distance. *Any moment now fear will get to me,* he thought. Then he wondered, *Which will be first, the attack or the fear?*

But there was no attack. As suddenly as they had come, the young men left. Unwilling to confess how frightened they had been, Néstor's friends stood motionless and listened. The car started up and drove off. Arévalo was the first to approach the other group.

"They wanted to work us over?" he asked.

"Not quite that," said the short young man. "But something similar."

"The thing is, nobody faces up to them. But he and I did," said the other young man.

"For the sake of *señor* Néstor, who was like a father to us."

"We convinced them that your group had already suffered its loss, in the person of *señor* Néstor."

"Who was like a father to you," said Rey.

"The truth is that nobody in this country is willing to risk his skin," said Vidal aggressively. "If any harm is done, it's always by accident. People always grasp at the first chance to back off."

"That's nothing to complain about," said Arévalo.

"It's not that simple, *señor* Vidal," said the short young man. "They declared these two gentlemen"—he pointed to Rey and Dante—"obviously belonged on the list of old people."

"And your grandmother," said Dante.

"They wanted to take them away," said the short young man. "For a little walk. But we pointed out that one of you hasn't a single grey hair, and that the other one still seems quite robust."

"Didn't I tell you this was a rat trap?" demanded Dante. "They wanted to take me away. And why? So they could pump me full of lead. People have gone mad. I tell you it's depressing to realize the way this country is filled with hatred."

"And this is the youth that's supposed to think for itself," commented Arévalo. "It thinks and acts like a herd of sheep."

"You're wrong," Rey told him. "It thinks and acts like a mob. A mob of pigs."

"But I thought we were supposed to be the pigs," said the man with the enormous hands.

"There's no place for the individual anymore." Arévalo's voice was without expression. "There's nothing left but animals that are born, breed and then die. Some of these animals happen to be endowed with a conscience the way others have wings or horns."

Fear, and perhaps anger, was working on them now like a stimulant. "It's horrible," said Dante. "More and more people, less and less room. Everyone fighting with everyone else. Doesn't it seem to you that we're on the brink of a mass slaughter?"

"Do you realize," Arévalo asked, "that the concepts of the soul and immortality are somehow old-fashioned, small-town concerns nowadays? And we've all moved from the small town to a swarming hive?"

"Wherever you look," said Dante, "you find nothing but malice and disorder. To give just one example, what do you think of the way women are dressing today? Isn't it the last straw? Isn't the end of the world just around the corner?"

Vidal had followed the conversation with interest, but now he suddenly lost patience. He went to have a last look at Néstor. *It's the least I can do,* he thought. *With his eyes closed, he doesn't look like a hen anymore. The poor guy looks good.* Shortly after thinking *poor guy,* he could feel tears starting down his cheeks.

XXIII

Monday, 30 June

Sitting bolt upright in his chair, Vidal rubbed his eyes and glanced around. A cold greyish light entered the room, casting shadows that emphasized the immobility of things. The impassive ticking of the clock mingled with the hum of the boys' voices and with Rey's snores, as he slept with his mouth contemptuously open. Arévalo was smoking, with a faraway look on his face; Dante was drowsing peacefully. The room was vaguely disordered with ashes and cigarette stubs scattered everywhere. From time to time Vidal thought of Néstor—for the process of forgetting had already begun—and little stabs of remorse pricked through his weariness. These memories gave way to others: he thought of his father's last days, remembering him—so near and yet now so far out of reach—in his bitter, fearful struggle with death. Every one of us is alone, powerless to help his fellow man. Vidal sensed the desolate certainty that any effort was vain. What had the essentially vain urge to talk that night been all about? When they were together, each one knew beforehand what the other was going to say. It was wrong to have kept on chattering that way in the presence of death—but he had kept on.

Only yesterday their lives had been untroubled; and suddenly the very condition of life itself had become intolerable. Suddenly, he longed to get away, longed, for the second or third time in these last few hours, to be outside. Everything he did that night he seemed compelled to do repeatedly.

He must have slipped imperceptibly from his meditations into sleep, for he saw before him the old woman weeping in the cab in front of the Plaza Las Heras. Néstor had died, he thought, because he, Vidal, had looked on that stricken face. With a start he became aware of a fellow who was white from top to toe—perhaps covered with flour—and who, with a pleasant smile, was offering him something wrapped in paper. It was one of the apprentices from Rey's shop, serving hot crescent-rolls and biscuits for breakfast. Probably he was afraid of waking the boss. But now the boss woke up in a fine mood and cheerfully invited his friends to come into the kitchen while he made coffee.

"What's so special about today?" asked Dante. "We're all in a good mood, don't you think?"

"But why, do you suppose?" Vidal asked.

"It's very simple, though you might not understand. I dreamed that the Excursionists had scored a sensational victory."

"Come on into the kitchen," said Rey again. "I have to get breakfast ready."

Dante grinned slyly. "After all these years we finally have the run of the house." It occurred to Vidal that a diminished sensibility protects the old, the way a shell protects the turtle.

"Come and sit down," said Rey cheerfully.

Vidal lagged behind, as though he meant to follow the others; but when they had left the room he turned to the door and walked out. It was broad daylight. He had gone only one block before he found his poncho uncomfortable. Indian summer had truly arrived at last. Up ahead, beyond a smouldering bonfire, a delivery man was going from door to door, leaving his newspapers. Vidal was feeling in his pocket for some change, when the man said, "I've no paper for you, grandpa." Was it merely that the man had no extra copies, he wondered, or was he refusing to sell a paper to an old man?

At Jimmy's the blinds were still closed. It was absurd, he told himself, but he felt uneasy. He must put this notion out of his mind, this idea that everybody in the street—first the milkman, then the night watchman, and now the woman scrubbing the doorstep of the house opposite—were looking at him with a barely concealed mixture of surprise and hostility. At last the door opened slightly, and Leticia's tiny head poked out.

"Is Jimmy at home?"

"I don't know. What time is it? He must be still asleep."

Her little round, close-set eyes were watching him. To indicate he was a friend of the family, he said, "I thought you worked by the day."

"I have a bed here, as of yesterday," she told him, with obvious satisfaction.

"You've heard about what a commotion there was last night? All of Jimmy's friends would feel much easier to know he was at home. Please don't wake him, but find out if you can."

The girl was going to leave him waiting outside on the doorstep; then, as though she had reconsidered, she let him in. By a narrow stairs they went down to the basement room, the scene of the chase he had watched so attentively the day before.

"Wait here," she said. "I'll be right back."

Please let him be there, thought Vidal. *I can't stand to have anything more go wrong.* In the ups and downs which chance deals out more or less impartially, he felt he was beginning to see a pattern. It said, beyond question, that fortune did not favor him.

In a moment Leticia returned. He looked at her, too impatient to wait for an answer. With a smile she finally said, "Only the niece is there, and I didn't wake her."

"So Jimmy's not home?"

"I'll wake the niece, if you like, and you can ask her."

"No, absolutely not."

The girl smiled as if she understood, and stared straight at him. "Care for some *maté?*"

"No, no thank you," he said hurriedly.

Though he climbed the stairs slowly, it seemed to him he was running. As he opened the door to the street he heard, from the basement, a sudden gasp for breath, followed by what he first took to be a sob, and then recognized as a burst of laughter.

XXIV

HE straightened his tie, adjusted his poncho, and set out at a jaunty step. *How quickly she was corrupted,* he thought. *No, put it another way. Yesterday she was being chased, today she chases after me.* He deplored the fact that such trivialities should be occupying his thoughts at a moment when he had just been furnished incontrovertible evidence—those were his exact words—that something had happened to Jimmy. But in his mind's eye he pictured the girl reaching out to him with her thick, roughened hands. Somebody—Jimmy perhaps or, more likely, Arévalo—had remarked that extreme ugliness can act as a powerful erotic stimulus: love, after all, is not far removed from madness. He tried to picture the girl as he might perhaps have seen her. His head swam, he felt close to fainting. *Disgraceful,* he muttered to himself. Reminding himself that he had had nothing to eat for what seemed like days, he headed for the bakery. He should have accepted Leticia's invitation to have some *maté,* even if *maté* might not have been all that she was offering. The moment he got home he would put water on to boil. Some *maté* and a few mouthfuls of bread would cure this inopportune weakness. He felt guilty about having left the wake.

There were no customers in the shop when he came in, only Rey's daughters. Out of sheer diffidence, he did not say hello.

"Six brioches, four crescent rolls, and a sugary bun."

"Did my father stay for the wake?" asked one of the girls.

"So they could get polished off all at once," said the other daughter.

Perhaps it was partly weariness, but he felt profoundly depressed. With his strength failing, his illusions gone, he felt he could no longer face life. Friendship had turned to indifference, love had shown itself sordid and false. Only hatred flourished. He had defended himself, and would go on defending himself (he felt no doubt on that score) against the attacks of the young; but as he came into Paunero Street he had a mental picture of his own hand holding a revolver to his temple. (And this was a possible solution, not to be lightly dismissed.) His response to this vision—which might be only the product of an acute but passing anxiety—was a protest, a protest against everything, but most of all against himself, for wanting to destroy what at first he had protected.

Madelón, who was scrubbing the pavement in front of her shop, motioned to him to wait. Setting her brush and pail inside, she closed the door and crossed the street. If what Madelón had to say was going to take much time, he thought, he would faint. He could not go much longer without his bread and his *maté*.

"I must talk to you," she said. "It's very important. I don't want us to be seen together. May I come to your room?"

They went in. He was about to lay his parcel down on the night table when it occurred to him that if he invited her to share it he might, without being rude, be able to have a slice of bread at once. He unwrapped the paper.

"Won't you have some?"

"At a time like this? How could you?" she protested, and burst into tears.

"What's the matter?" he asked.

She seized his hands (her own were damp) and drew him close to her. He recognized the smells of laundry soap, bleach, wet clothes and hair. "My darling," he heard her say.

A whiff of her breath told him she had not yet had breakfast. As her hands gripped him, he had a close-up view of yellowish, sweaty skin covered with moles, and stubby fingernails thickly coated with red polish. Not without pride he told himself that, after Nélida, he could not possibly have anything to do with Madelón.

On the pretext of wanting to speak to her, he contrived to push her slightly away. "What's the matter?"

"I have something very important to tell you," she said again, and embraced him vigorously.

Locked into a position that was uncomfortable, painful almost (because a sturdy forearm was forcing him to tilt his head to one side), he wondered why it was that women were chasing him today, throwing themselves at him just when he was most depressed and in his poorest form. Was it not further proof of the sheer contrariness of things? Another possible explanation, and less pessimistic, was that things happen in series. But was Madelón really offering herself to him, or did she want to tell him something?

As though she had read his mind, Madelón explained, "Huguito told me that his nephew, who knows everything that's going on, has said that . . . Oh, I just can't believe it!"

"What did he say?" asked Vidal, with barely concealed impatience.

"He said you've been singled out and you're to be the next victim."

He felt a surge of resentment for the woman, as if she were responsible for what he had just heard. How stupid, he thought, to suppose that after she had brought this piece of news, he should feel any desire to take her in his arms. At the same time, he noted she was squeezing him below the waist with an urgency that could not be mistaken. Objectively—but at the same time suffering the agony of a man who knows that at any moment he will be drawn into action—he wondered what would happen next, what was he going to do with this woman panting in his arms. Because he could not forget the old Madelón, and because he was compassionate by nature, he disliked the idea of rejecting her. But in such a situation, he wondered, would his will determine what his conduct would be? He tried to imagine her as she once had been; his eyes and nose persisted in perceiving her as she was now.

Stalling for time, he said, "These Bogliolos, the uncle and the nephew . . ."

"Forget them," Madelón advised him. "Doesn't danger excite you? It does me."

The door opened and a voice said, "Excuse me."

The two words were enough to express to the fullest Nélida's sense of outrage. Her face was strangely livid, blotched with crimson; her eyes gleamed feverishly. A moment later she had gone, slamming the door.

It was a catastrophe for Vidal and his first impulse was to place the blame squarely on Madelón; but before he could speak, it occurred to him that she might view things in a different light. So he said merely, "It's impossible to be at ease in this room. With Isidorito right next door, and somebody always barging in . . ."

"You can always lock the door."

"Yes of course, but right now I'm as nervous as a cat. You know what I'm like when I'm nervous. I swear I'm no good for anything."

"Don't exaggerate."

"Besides, it's too late. I have to get back to the wake. I like to do things at the right time and place. Why don't we get together some evening?"

Protesting feebly, Madelón proposed they set a date for their rendezvous, offered him the shop as a hiding place: he must not forget Hugito's warning. He managed to push her gently out the door. Alone at last, he heaved a sigh of relief, as though he were among his friends. But the relief was not genuine: on the contrary, he was beginning to have doubts about the true reasons for his sudden withdrawal. He now began to fear he had behaved rudely to Madelón, and dishonestly to Nélida. This last concern he dismissed, for there were no grounds for his supposing there was anything more than simple friendship between him and the girl. As for the motives underlying his abrupt withdrawal, they would doubtless return later to nag at him.

He decided to forego his *maté* (it was too late) and, munching on a crust of bread, he left his room, hoping not to run into Madelón in the street. He would make a stop at the bathroom first. In the second courtyard he ran into Nélida, who turned away from him. Deeply distressed, he tried to stammer out some explanation, but this was cut short when Antonia appeared.

XXV

WHEN he reached Néstor's house, he found the conversation had shifted to the subject of certain old people who—more for the fun of it than out of real malice—had been pitched into the ritual St. Peter and St. Paul bonfires. There had been four or five partial cremations in their own neighborhood. The victims attended to their burns in Garaventa's pharmacy; all except one, with second-degree burns, who was treated at Fernández Hospital. They mentioned cases of kidnapping, which was a fairly new feature of the war. For the first time, observed Vidal, the profit motive was appearing.

"I hope to God it's only a case of kidnapping with Jimmy," he said. "I don't know why, but that was the first thing I thought of . . ."

"And now you're afraid of something worse?" asked Arévalo.

"With these brutes, you can never . . ."

"The important thing is to keep calm," said the man with the big hands.

"Calm! We'll keep them calm with our fists!" Rey bellowed, menacingly. "Just find where they've got Jimmy locked up, and I swear I'll get him out."

They discussed informing the police, weighed the pros and cons, considered the risks and the probable futility. Vidal nearly said, "Maybe they'll let him go if he's just been kidnapped," but checked himself. It would have meant answering a lot of troublesome questions about what he meant.

They went back to talking about Néstor and the imminent burial service. Why was his son still not there? The man with the pointed face said, "I think it's highly irregular."

"Youth." The man with the enormous hands spoke with his customary indulgence. "Youth has its own affairs to attend to. Haven't we all heard, 'Let the dead bury . . .'?"

"Your grandmother," said Dante, whose hearing seemed to have improved.

"Before we go to the cemetery," Rey proposed, "why don't we circle the block, carrying the coffin? It's the custom, in cases of death by violence. With Néstor's body on our shoulders, we'll offer the enemy a united front."

Vidal glanced at the two strangers, first the one with the big hands, next the one with the sharp nose; surely they would raise objections. Both kept silent. After a pause, in which the big man could be heard shifting in his chair, Dante said, "I don't believe we're in any position to antagonize people."

"Least of all when we're carrying the coffin," said Arévalo.

How shrewd the two strangers had been, thought Vidal: convinced that common sense would triumph, they had had the wit not to endanger the cause by pleading it themselves. When it became apparent that all of them, except Rey, were in favor of moderation, the man with the enormous hands pointed out, "Besides, surely it would be irresponsible of us to involve the funeral-home assistants."

"Innocent employees," the sharp-featured man put in.

There was an immediate reaction; for a moment the moderates were in danger of being defeated. The arrival of Néstor's son at this point diverted the conversation and, in the end, saved them all; the project was abandoned. With great eloquence the young man thanked them all for coming; such a magnificent demonstration of loyalty was more than ample compensation for his distress at being unable to stand watch by his father's body. The police—mere cogs, after all, in the wheels of a vast, unfeeling machine—were concerned solely with bureaucratic routine. Intent on procedures and interrogations, they had been entirely indifferent to a son's grief.

Arévalo spoke to Vidal in a strange whisper. "Don't tell me you're going to cry."

"Poor fellow, I feel sorry for him."

"Do you think he was mixed up in it?" Rey asked.

"If they detained him for so long, right in the thick of this war," said Arévalo, "his behavior at the stadium must have been absolutely monstrous."

XXVI

VIDAL was allowed no time to recover his composure. The departure for the cemetery was announced, and there was a sudden bustle of activity in every part of the house. It was an effort for him to hold back his tears, for suddenly the most trivial relection seemed acutely painful. What affected him most was the sight of *doña* Regina, disheveled and intent, drifting about as if she were being transported by someone else. Turning away he saw Dante, in a fit of childlike excitement, saying over and over, "Remember, boys, we mustn't get separated. Stay together, stay together."

"Deaf and blind," Vidal thought. "With the hide of a rhinoceros. Old people are nothing but animals."

"The main thing," said Arévalo, giving a wink reminiscent of Jimmy's, "is to make sure undesirables don't slip in."

"Who's going with Néstor's son?" asked Rey.

"The four of us stick together," said Dante.

"We know," Vidal muttered, or merely thought.

For the last time he glanced back at the house: it looked desolate. As if in a trance, he got into the car. During the whole drive he sat with his face to the window, trying not to betray the emotion he was unable to conceal. To his own surprise he heard himself saying, "Everything looks different, viewed from the hearse."

"Your grandmother," said Dante, who seemed to understand every word this morning, as though he had at last bought a hearing-aid. "We're not all laid out in a hearse yet."

Driving along Libertador, they circled the Spanish Monument. "My God but I'm old," sighed Arévalo. "Shall I tell you one of my earliest memories? I remember being on this avenue—it was still called Alvear then—and watching the open touring cars go by, with horns in the shape of brass snakes. Some of them were painted in a basket-weave design, black and yellow. Where have they gone, those huge Renaults, and the Hispano-Suizas, and the Delaunay-Bellevilles?"

Dante's response was a sigh of nostalgia. "They say there used to be a lagoon where Malabia Street is now."

"And another one across from Guadalupe Chapel," said Arévalo.

Early spring hung in the air. Vidal took off his poncho and complained, "It's so hot!"

"It's the humidity," Dante explained.

"Have you heard anything," Rey wanted to know, "about this Old People's March that's being planned? A well-timed demonstration, and probably an effective one."

"Now really," said Arévalo. "Can you imagine what it would be like? We'd turn the whole city against us. A spectacle right out of Dante."

Jimmy, thought Vidal, would have stressed that last phrase to get a rise out of Dante, but the rest of them were weary of that particular joke.

"A proper doomsday spectacle," said Dante. "Don't you see that? These crazy, abominable things going on everywhere—if they aren't a sign that the end of the world is near, then what do they mean?"

"There comes a day," said Arévalo, "when every old man decides the end of the world is at hand. At times I lose patience myself . . ."

"That's enough!" Rey cut in. "Are we supposed to be encouraging these young ruffians with their ridiculous pretensions?"

"Anyway, old people are getting tired out," said Vidal.

"And are you going to tell me," Dante demanded, "that these

crazy styles the women are wearing aren't the last straw? That they aren't a sign everything is going to pieces, that the world's coming to an end?"

They were driving along Juan B. Justo now, near the Pacific Railway Station. "There's no way you can defend old people," said Arévalo. "All you can do is appeal to sentiment: think of all they've done for us, they have feelings just as we have, they suffer and so forth. You probably don't know how the Eskimos and the Lapps get rid of their old folks?"

"You told us all about it," said Dante.

"You see?" said Arévalo, wheezing. "We're repeating ourselves. All old people are as alike as peas in a pod, all in the same boat, all with the same hardening of the arteries."

"The same what?" asked Dante. "I can't hear you when you speak with your mouth closed. Look up ahead, all of you. When I was a boy I lived in the next block. They've already knocked the house down."

Vidal thought of the house he had lived in as a child: the courtyard, with the wisteria; the dog, Vigilante; the sound of the trolley car in the night, screeching around the bend before it picked up speed and went roaring past the door.

"You'll never guess where there was a dairy farm," said Arévalo. "On Montevideo, just a stone's throw from Alvear. There was a livery stable on the corner."

"A what?" asked Dante.

"Do you remember, Rey?" Vidal asked. "There was a woman living next to your bakery who was a hundred years old."

"*Doña* Juana. She was still there when I had the place enlarged. The very soul of hospitality. At her table even your local Argentine cuisine was dazzling. Her beef stews, her pies! I have her to thank, too, for teaching me Spanish history. It was back when she saw Princess Isabel, who was visiting here, drive past in her carriage. *Doña* Juana had two granddaughters, a homely one and a pretty one, both with freckles."

"Pilar and Celia," said Vidal. "Celia was the pretty one, she died young. I had a crush on her."

"Whatever became of the time," asked Dante, "when women used to run after us?"

Shall I tell them or not? thought Vidal.

"It's gone forever," said Rey.

"I'd be surprised if it ever returned," said Arévalo, phlegmatically.

"I can hardly bring myself to believe it," Vidal said to them, "but today two women made advances to me. To me, mind you."

"What happened?" Rey asked.

"Nothing. They were too ugly." (*And besides,* he said, but only to himself, *there's Nélida.*)

"Are you sure it's not that you're too old?" Dante asked him. "In our young days we weren't so particular."

That's true, thought Vidal. Villa Crespo was behind them now. A prolonged silence fell, broken by Rey. "How quiet we all are. What are you thinking, Arévalo?"

"Something laughable. I just had a sort of vision."

"Just now?"

"Just now. I seemed to see a well, which stood for the past, and people, animals, and things were falling into it."

"Yes," said Vidal, "it makes you dizzy."

"So does the future. I think of it as a cliff turned upside down, with new people and new things appearing at the edge as though they were here to stay, but they topple over and disappear into the void."

"You see?" said Dante. "Not all old people are blithering idiots. Some of them are even intelligent."

"That's why they call us owls," said Arévalo.

"Pigs," Rey corrected him.

"Pigs or owls. The owl symbolizes philosophy. Intelligent, but repulsive."

They drove into the cemetery, then got out at the chapel. At the end of the service they returned to their automobiles. The one he and his friends occupied, Vidal noted, was the third and last in line. It was hot. They began the slow trip back in the car. Arévalo asked, "What were you saying, Vidal, about a pretty girl who died young?"

"Her name was Celia. I was crazy about her."

Without warning, the car braked. The windshield cracked, and suddenly turned completely opaque. Vidal opened the door and got out to see what had happened. There was an unnatural stillness, as though not just the car but the whole world had come to a stop. The door of the first car swung open; he saw the man with the enormous hands climb out and, in a touching gesture, raised those hands to his face. Beyond the flower-decked hearse ahead, a crowd of people were laughing, dancing, crouching with their bodies twisted, springing up again. Then he saw that the man's face was covered with blood, and recognized in the contortions of the people beyond the motions of a pitcher winding up. They were throwing stones.

"We're caught in the rat trap!" Dante wailed.

Stones were falling all around him. Somebody shouted hoarsely, "Run!"

Vidal didn't hesitate; he started to run. When he was out of breath, he threw himself down and crawled to shelter behind a gravestone. The close contact with this ground and this grass was distasteful. When he stood up, he was shivering. Another stone landed very near, and he began to run again, for as long as he could. Then he slowed down to a walk, thinking that he must not lose his way in this vast cemetery. He became aware of slight taps, like fingers drumming, on his neck and shoulders. Drops. Thick, heavy drops. It had started to rain. "A dirty rain," he thought, "mingling with sweat." Stumbling and falling repeatedly, he hurried as far as the exit on Jorge Newbery Street, and finally, now limping, he reached Corrientes Avenue after crossing the Los Andes Park. *There's a word for this,* he said to himself. He was too weary to look for the word, but presently it came to him. *Humiliating. How humiliating.* He thought: *I'll stop the first cab.* But several came along and continued on their way, as though they had not seen his motions. He went into a bar and propped his elbows on the counter.

"A cold beer and two ham sandwiches," he said.

Wiping the sink with a rag, the man said, "If you wish, but I don't recommend it. Things are a little tense."

He did not want to appear stubborn; he thanked the bartender and turned to the door. *It's only natural, it's only to be expected,* he thought. *Humiliation, of course. That is, if you're old.*

XXVII

SINCE outside he faced a downpour, he turned back to the bartender with a questioning look on his face. The latter, who had probably anticipated the gesture, jerked his head roughly toward the street. Vidal walked as far as Dorrego. If he stayed close to the buildings, he would get only one shoulder soaked. Three or four times he waved his hand to signal a taxi; none stopped. He was already on the stairs leading to the subway when it occurred to him someone might yield to temptation and push him under a train. Confused by fatigue and weakness, he added, *Besides, it doesn't take me very near home.* Back on the street again, he noted that what with the rain on the outside and the sweat inside, his clothes were soaked. *Luckily I'm not old yet,* he thought to himself. *Lots of people, with less cause than this, would have contracted double pneumonia or chronic bronchitis.* He tried a tentative cough. Although the 93 bus would take him close to his home, he did not dare to get on it: among such a busload of passengers he could very likely count on at least one aggressor. Just when it seemed that the only possible solution, however unthinkable, was to undertake the interminable journey on foot, the rain stopped. Taking this as a good sign, he set out on the prodigious march. He had lost count by now of the hours he had gone without food and sleep.

If he should be attacked on one of the boulevards, there would likely be passersby who would come to the rescue; but at the same time he would be more exposed than on some deserted side-street where he could spot trouble from a distance . . . Coming into Bonpland Street, he observed that a wind had sprung up from the south, and that it had turned cool again. *A proper fate for an old fool,* he thought, *to escape from real danger and then die of a chill.* As he reached Soler, he saw a group of boys; though they might be harmless, he gave them a wide berth, crossing the railroad tracks at Paraguay. An uneven paving-stone tripped him and sent him sprawling. He lay on the ground, trembling, exhausted. Struggling to his feet he felt sure he was forgetting something very important he had just thought of a few seconds earlier. *I nearly fell asleep walking,* he thought. *Terrible.* He went on and at last managed to catch a taxi at Plaza Güemes, an old taxi with an old man at the wheel who listened carefully while Vidal gave him the address. He lowered his flag. "You did the right thing, sir. After a certain age, it's best not to pick out a cab with a young driver."

"Why?"

"Haven't you heard? One of their favorite sports is robbing old people and then just tossing them out."

Vidal had been almost lying back against the seat. He straightened up now, and leaned forward. "No one can tell me there's any scientific justification for this war. It's all the work of a bunch of hoodlums."

"You're quite right, sir. The old-style Argentine is a man who prizes friendship. These young kids like to think of themselves as big-game hunters, and so they set out to hunt us."

"You can't feel safe for a minute. The worst thing is to live in constant fear of a surprise attack."

"That's what I was going to say. Suppose there are too many useless old people around. Why not gather them in some suitable place and exterminate them by modern methods?"

"Wouldn't the cure be worse than the disease? I'm thinking about possible abuses."

"I suppose you're right. There's a lot of abuse of power in the government. The telephone system, for instance."

Vidal paid the fare and got out. He may never have been wearier. He thought of his friends, hoping none of them had been hit with a stone as the man with the big hands had been. Intent first of all on making good his escape, then on getting back home, he had completely forgotten them. *Com-plate-ly forgotten, as poor Néstor would have said.* The memory stirred him. Did he still have the strength left to make it to Dante's, or to Rey's bakery? *Arévalo is a queer bird. Nobody I know of has ever set foot in his home. Not even Jimmy, who's so inquisitive.* This last observation was made for the benefit of those who were listening to him discourse in a dream.

XXVIII

Though he no longer had strength left even to stay on his feet, he still put off the moment of decision. Should he go to bed, or go out again to check up on his friends? First he would have some *maté* to restore his energy. He was waiting for the water to boil, munching on some bread, when Nélida appeared.

She looked him straight in the eye. "Forgive me for not knocking. A bad habit."

"Not at all. Why do you say that?"

"I always pick the wrong moment. But I wanted to warn you."

"To warn me of what, Nélida?"

"That there are certain hypocrites who give you a friendly smile and then, when your back is turned, denounce you if it suits their purpose. A lady friend of yours, who talks to Bogliolo regularly, must know perfectly well that the nephew . . ."

"Yes, Nélida, I know. That friend came to warn me."

"And while she was about it, she . . . They all come here because they're crazy about you."

"Don't say that, Nélida. Madelón is not crazy about me, and she's not the kind of lady friend you think."

"Madelón! If there's nothing between you, why does Bogliolo allow his nephew to turn your name in? Do you know why? Because you could take over his place with her any time you wanted to."

"No. I'm not taking over anyone's place."

"I wonder what you see in that old woman."

"Nothing, Nélida. Would you be angry if I said something? I'm dying for some sleep. I was going to go to bed right now. I was just about to undress."

"Who's stopping you?"

"But, Nélida," he protested, and then, with a resigned shrug, he turned off the stove.

"But what?"

He watched her as she sat on the edge of the bed, calmly removing her shoes and hose, marveling at her easy grace as she stripped off the nylons and tossed them onto a chair. Gratefully, he wondered, "Is it possible I can be so lucky?" She stood up; as though she were alone, she looked at herself for an instant in the mirror, and then, in a single movement—at least so it seemed to him—uncovered her nakedness, so white in the shadows of the room. Trembling before this revelation, he heard her voice very near, "Idiot. Idiot." She held him close, caressed him, kissed him, until he pushed her away a little, to look at her.

"Do you know something?" he asked. "I was dying for you, dying, and I'm such a fool I'd never have worked up the courage to tell you."

Her open mouth provided a second revelation. They fell into each other's arms; unable to speak, he pressed her closer to him. It was like drowning in a field of lavender. After a while he drew quickly away from her. She slapped him violently.

"Why?" she wailed. "Why?"

"Why did you hit me? I just wanted . . ."

"That's my business." But her anger was short-lived.

"Has it all been a dream? I can't be sure, I keep dozing off all the time."

"And is this a dream too?" Nélida laughed and touched him on the cheek. "Shall we go to sleep?"

"Aren't Antonia and her mother expecting you?"

"I'm in the midst of moving, they'll think I stayed at my aunt's."

"You're moving?"

"Didn't you know? The night before last poor Aunt Paula

died, the one who baked the cakes, remember? I always spoke of 'my aunts,' but the truth is there was only one left. I was advised to take her apartment at once, before anybody else got in."

"Is it far?" he asked uneasily.

"No, it's on Guatemala, just off Julián Alvarez."

"My old neighborhood."

"Not really?"

"I was born on Paraguay Street. The nicest thing about the house was the patio, with the wisteria. I had a dog named Vigilante. But I don't want to bore you with all that. Antonia and her mother are going to miss you."

"Oh, I don't know. It was an intolerable situation. Maybe poor Antonia would just as soon have nobody around, because, after all, it is her mother. The old woman has become impossible to live with. Age has changed her so that she's actually turned into a sort of disgusting man. Everybody calls her the Dragoon. I'm worried, though, about her little granddaughters. But, my poor darling, I'm keeping you from your sleep."

His eyes were closing, but he could not bear to break off the conversation . . . Years ago, perhaps, he had had a sensation of well-being comparable to this. *But,* he thought, *it's a luxury I'm not used to now, and I'm not going to waste it.*

XXIX

He was awakened by a noise which he took to be rifle fire: he was shooting at an owl. He remembered the dream clearly: he was in a shelter, a little stone hut which (they had assured him) was solidly built and quite safe. Looking around, like a satisfied owner inspecting his property, he glanced up: the roof was missing. Through the opening enraged owls swooped down on him, then, with a clumsy flapping of wings, mounted into the air only to return to the attack. He had fired on the owl who was hooting the loudest . . . Fully awake now, he turned over on his left side: Nélida was there. *What a life I've led these last years,* he thought, *to have dreams like this with her beside me.* Watching as she lay sleeping, he thought of something quite unimportant, but which pleased him because it belonged to his youth: with a woman, he had always been the first to fall asleep, and the first to waken. How long had it been now, since he had thought of that?

Like a student reviewing a lesson, he went over, point by point, everything that had happened since the moment Nélida had come into the room. He was glad he had resisted the temptation to ask a question which would have been untimely, perhaps even fatal: *What about your fiancé?* There was a certain moment when, suffering qualms on behalf of this unknown man, he had very nearly asked the question. If he did now, it would be because the possessive instinct compelled him to do so. Amused, he thought, *When it comes to making demands, a man is quick to learn.*

Suddenly he felt he understood that the act of love explained the entire universe. With the humility and pride of someone who understands that the greatest prizes simply drop into our laps, not as a reward for our own merits, but just because they have to go to someone, he told himself that last night he had been one of the winners. Feeling the need to share his exultation, he moved closer to the girl; he looked at her earnestly for a long moment, saying slowly to himself, *Incredibly lovely.* Very carefully, as though his main concern was not to waken her, he took her in his arms again.

A few minutes later they were lying on their backs, talking comfortably. "I'm keeping you from sleeping again," said Nélida.

"No, it's not you. I'm just hungry. I haven't eaten for two days."

"What can I fix for you?"

"There's almost nothing here."

"I'll get dressed and bring something from Antonia's."

"No, don't go. We've got bread, and *maté,* and dried fruit, and maybe a bar of chocolate. But the chocolate is Isidorito's, and he'll be angry if we eat it. When he gets hungry, he feels faint."

Nélida laughed, paying no attention. "What about the faint feeling we've had?"

She switched on the lamp and stood up. From the bed he pointed out where things were, and watched her move about the room, still naked.

"I'll put fresh water on to boil," she said, emptying the pot. "Do you know what I dreamed? That we'd gone hunting, you and I, and your dog Vigilante."

"I can't believe it. I had a dream, too, about hunting some kind of enormous bird."

Delightedly, they agreed that this was a miraculous coincidence.

"I've heard about you," she told him. "From a woman I met yesterday at my aunt Paula's. Her name is Nélida too."

"You don't mean the Nélida who used to live here in this house?"

It was indeed the same one. "You seem to remember her very well," commented Nélida.

Perhaps to avoid showing too lively an interest in an old flame, he asked "Is Carmen living with her?"

"Don't be silly. She's getting married any day now."

After a moment of confusion, he realized that this Carmen must be Nélida's daughter, but he did not explain that it was her mother, not her daughter, that he asked about. Once more he was on the point of asking, *What about your fiancé?* But he checked himself, afraid it might be the wrong time.

"Here's a feast to put new life into us," said Nélida.

They laughed all through the meal. *Won't we wake up Isidorito with all this racket?* Vidal wondered. *Won't he walk in and find out Nélida is in my room?* Then he stopped worrying. *Unless I'm mistaken, it makes no difference to her. And she's right. What matters is to remember last night. The best night of my life.* At once he felt annoyed with himself for already reliving what he was living still, for viewing the present as though it were the past; annoyed also at the realization that it was a kind of withdrawal from Nélida. He thought too, *Lately I've fallen into the bad habit of wondering whether everything that happens to me isn't happening for the last time. It's as if I deliberately wanted to ruin everything with my gloomy attitude.*

"Why don't you come and live with me?" Nélida asked him.

His first impulse was to reject the idea, simply because it caught him unawares; then, to his surprise, he began to accept it; and in the end he felt it was necessary to make it clear that he would meet the expenses (which protected his self-esteem, though he did not ask what these expenses might amount to, nor did he calculate how much money he could count on). The girl paid scant heed, and listened with such openly expressed impatience that Vidal thought, *I must sound terribly old-fashioned*. Uncertain just how he had blundered ,he retreated into silence. But he could not resist the overpowering urge to ask, finally, the question he had so frequently repressed: "What about your fiancé?"

Probably, he thought, *another mistake of the same kind, that would demonstrate the hopelessness of bridging the two generations.*

"Does it matter so much to you?"

"Very much," he answered, bravely.

"Good. I was afraid maybe it didn't. Don't worry, I'll tell him it's all over. I've chosen you."

Elated and triumphant at hearing these words, which were so precious to him—all that a lover could hope for, in words or actions, had been granted to him this day—he was leading Nélida back to the bed when there was a knock at the door. He put on his old brown overcoat and went to see who it was.

XXX

"To the attic, man, to the attic!" It was Faber, all excited, poking his grizzled head through the half-opened door.

"What's going on?" Vidal asked, moving to block Faber's view, so that he would not catch sight of Nélida.

"Didn't you hear the shots? It was just like in the movies. You must be a sound sleeper, *don* Isidro. I may be half deaf, but when I'm asleep I can hear a pin drop."

He pushed forward, trying to come in, as if he suspected something, or had perhaps caught a glimpse of Nélida. Vidal kept one hand firmly on the latch and leaned against the door jamb. "I have no intention of going to the attic," he announced.

"When they found the front door locked," Faber went on, "—the manager has a padlock on it now—they tried to blast the lock open with their pistols. Fortunately, along came one of those patrols that make such a big show of preserving law and order. But they promised to be back, *don* Isidro. If you don't believe me, ask the others. Everybody heard it."

"I'm telling you that I'm staying right here in my room. In the first place, I don't consider myself an old man."

"You're perfectly right, but it's better to err on the side of caution."

"Besides, I'm not afraid of them. Why should I be afraid of the kids in this neighborhood, when I've known them practically since the day they were born? And they know me too, and they know I'm not an old man. You can believe what I'm saying. They've told me themselves."

"But the ones who said they'd be back aren't from the neighborhood. They're from the Associated City Employees. They've requisitioned some trucks from the Dog Pound, and they're driving up and down the main streets, ferreting old people out of their hovels. And then they put them in cages and ride them around. Just to make fun of them is my guess."

"And what do they do to them afterwards?" asked Nélida. She was behind Vidal. *Faber must surely be able to see her arms,* he thought.

"There are people who say that they shove them into the gas chambers where they exterminate mad dogs. On the other hand, a fellow-countryman of the Dog Pound manager told him for a fact that they open the cages when they get to San Pedrito, and then they chase them with whips off toward Flores cemetery."

"Shut the door," Nélida ordered.

Vidal shut the door and turned to her.

"He's crazy. I'm not going up into the attic with the old people."

"Look," she advised him, "if I were in your place, I'd hide out tonight and slip away the first thing in the morning."

"Where would I go?"

"To Guatemala Street. You're coming to my place, agreed? Just try not to attract attention, and once you're there, they'll need a wizard to find you."

He had flatly turned down the proposal that he should hide in the attic, but now, viewed as a part of Nélida's plan, the idea seemed worth considering. For the moment, if he was not to attract attention (as she had advised), he could not take much with him. Which amounted to saying there was nothing final about this move. With the excuse that he was saving his life, he could enjoy the experience of living for a week with a woman. It would not be easy, perhaps, to come back. Maybe by that time he would have formed a new habit, the habit of living with Nélida, as opposed to the old habit of living with his son (which amounted to living alone). But he could not think so far ahead.

He took her in his arms and said cheerfully, "If it's a firm invitation, I'll be at your house tomorrow."

"You'll never get there if I don't give you the address. Here, take the keys, so you won't have to ring the bell and wait around. I'll get someone to let me in."

The keys were in one of her pockets. They hunted for pencil and paper, which they finally found, and she wrote down the address. Without stopping to read it, Vidal put it away.

XXXI

Climbing the steep, rickety stairs again, he knew he had not been mistaken: it was an humiliation to go into the attic. When he arrived there, the low roof, the smells, the dirt, the feathers confirmed his impression. At the end of a kind of tunnel—the attic ran the full length of the left wing—he could see a lighted candle and two figures outlined against the darkness, whom he recognized as Faber and the custodian. He crawled over to them.

"Here comes the prodigal son," said Faber. "Bogliolo is still missing, though."

"He won't be here," the custodian replied. "He's gone into hiding with the upholsterer's daughter. Now that her father is dead, she entertains her men friends in the house."

"Lots of men are hiding out with their mistresses," said Faber.

"Yes, and just as proud as can be. But since the first thing these people check on is who's sleeping with whom, they can locate them any time they please."

Probably neither of them, thought Vidal, had spoken with deliberate malice. To show them—or perhaps to show himself—that none of this affected him, he joined in the conversation. "It looks as though this war of the pigs, or of the old people, has broken out again, after a relatively quiet spell."

"It's in the last stages, though." Faber spoke in the high-pitched voice that had been a habit with him for some time now. "The young people are losing heart."

"They're ineffectual," Vidal said. "Nothing happens in this war, it's all just threats. I know what I'm talking about. I've been involved once or twice with them."

"It may be all right for you to talk like that," said the custodian solemnly, "but they killed your friend Néstor, didn't they? And your friend Jimmy disappeared. Let's pray he shows up alive."

"The young ones are losing heart," said Faber again. "In the near future, if we still have a democratic form of government, it's the old ones who will run it. It's a question of simple mathematics, you understand. Majority of votes. All right, what do statistics show us? People nowadays don't die at fifty, they die at eighty, and tomorrow it will be at a hundred. All right, then. At that rate, just think how the numbers of older people will increase, and imagine the weight their opinion will have in public affairs. The dictatorship of the proletariat has had its day, and the dictatorship of the old is destined to replace it."

Gradually his face darkened. "What is it?" asked the custodian. "You look upset."

"Frankly, I was thinking I should have gone to the washroom before I came up here. You know what I mean?"

"I certainly do. The same problem has been on my mind for a while now."

"To be honest, I can't think of anything else," Vidal chimed in.

They burst out laughing and slapped each other on the back, falling into a mood of camaraderie. "Don't jolt me like that," the custodian begged, "or I'm done for."

"Watch out for the candle," said Faber, straightening it.

"If that pile of crates catches fire, we'll save the youngsters a lot of trouble."

"It's nothing to laugh about."

"Couldn't we risk a quick trip to the washroom?" Faber suggested.

"Impossible, on account of the young people in the house," the custodian replied. "Everybody's been told that we've left. If the others caught sight of us, we'd be putting people on the spot."

"Well, then, there's nothing to do," said Faber, laughing until the tears came, "but what babies do."

"Isn't there some likely place around here we could use?"

"Perhaps behind those crates at the back," said Vidal.

"Isn't that right over Bogliolo's room?"

"I couldn't say for sure," Vidal told him.

"Oh, now I understand," cried the custodian. "You're the one responsible for that damp spot on the ceiling. Well, now the three of us can make another one together."

Shaking with laughter—they kept bursting into loud guffaws, in spite of themselves—they managed to crawl over to the spot Vidal had pointed out. And there they remained briefly.

"Unless he rents a boat," Faber predicted, "he's going to drown."

As they crawled back, the custodian whispered in Vidal's ear, "His voice is changing. It's an adolescent's voice."

"It's like a duck quacking," said Vidal.

Abruptly they hushed, alarmed by noises below: loud whispers, jostling bodies, a rough male voice shouting some obscenity.

"My God, what's that?" asked Faber, in his quavering falsetto. He got no answer from them.

Heavy steps lumbered slowly up the creaking stairway. When the huge bulk loomed before him, Vidal felt truly afraid. He did not recognize immediately who it was. It was only when the little girl bringing up the rear arrived with her lantern, that he saw that this enormous, bloated, barrel-shaped bulk, brown as an Indian, white hair flying wild, was *doña* Dalmacia. She stood in the gloom, her rolling eyes filled with rage.

"Who are they?" she demanded.

"The custodian, Faber, and Vidal," her granddaughter told her.

Doña Dalmacia's face expressed supreme contempt. "Three sissies. Some little kids throw a scare into them, and they run off and hide. Listen, you bunch of fairies, I wanted to stay downstairs. Let them come after me if they like, I can knock them flat with one push. But my daughter sent me up here. That's because she's stupid and besides she thinks I'm blind."

A silence fell over the attic. "What is she doing now?" Vidal asked.

"She's forgotten about us," Faber told him. "She's playing with her granddaughter."

"I can't understand how they can leave the child with her," the custodian said. "The woman's turned into a fierce old hag. It's disgusting. But that's the sort of trick old age can play on you."

XXXII

Tuesday, 1 July

The appearance of *doña* Dalmacia had clearly had a depressing effect. Nobody said a word. It must have been late at night and at this stage of the war the days were exhausting, marked as they were by trying incidents. In the shadowy silence, Vidal fell asleep. He dreamed that he had knocked over the candle and the attic was ablaze, and that he himself, a victim along with the others, approved this purification by fire. Circumstances in the dream that he could not recall now led him to hope that the young people would triumph. He summed it up in a phrase which seemed to him quite suitable: *Since I have lived as a young man, I consent to allow the old man in me to die.* The effort of pronouncing the words, and perhaps the sound of them on his lips, roused him.

He must have remembered, even if not consciously, that on another occasion he had awakened in this attic, doubled up with lumbago; for the first thing he did was to try out some movements to test the limberness of his back. He discovered he felt no pain whatever.

"Always the first to wake up," he thought, with some pride. In the first light of dawn that was sifting through the skylight, he saw Faber and the custodian. *They look like a couple of breathing corpses,* he thought, surprised to find that sometimes the mere act of breathing can be disgusting to watch. He very nearly stumbled over the little girl. With her eyes half open, the whites showing, she wore the dazed look of a woman about to faint. A few feet beyond, the old woman lay slumped in a shapeless mass.

On the stairs he suddenly felt weak and giddy; he told himself he must have something to eat. For years, perhaps ever since childhood, he had been subject to dizzy spells when he had gone without food. Downstairs now, he paused, one hand on the banister. Not a sound. People were still asleep, but he had no time to lose; they would be stirring shortly.

Though his room was still cold and dark, he was struck once again, as he had been so many times in this past week, by the peaceful appearance of things. Depressed as he was, he wondered if this might not be a bad sign. He found himself looking at these objects, laid out for his own use, as though he had returned from some long voyage, and was watching them from outside, through a window.

He washed, put on his best clothes, wrapped up some handkerchiefs and a change of underwear in a newspaper. At the last minute he thought of the keys and the scrap of paper Nélida had given him. They were all in the pocket of his other suit. Beneath the address (and the instructions: third door, up the stairs, door E, follow the corridor, up the little stairway to the landing, apartment number 5) she had written: "I'll be waiting!" *How important little attentions like these can be in a man's life,* he thought. Then it occurred to him that he should leave Isidorito a note explaining his absence. He did not know what to say. He couldn't put down the truth, and it would have been impossible to disguise it. Moreover, he didn't have time to waste. He ended up writing: "A friend has invited me to spend three or four days in the country. Things are calmer at his place. Take care of yourself." Before he left he added: "I haven't given details, in case this should fall into the wrong hands."

On his way to the bathroom (for a while, at least, he wouldn't have that to worry about at Nélida's), he passed the youngest of *doña* Dalmacia's granddaughters, who probably did not even see him: her main concern was to avoid stepping on the cracks between the paving stones. Except for the child, he saw no one. In the street, which was still deserted, he glanced up curiously at the windows of the upholsterer's shop. If he had surprised Bogliolo standing in one of them, he would have felt neither jealousy nor resentment, but rather a kind of masculine solidarity. Perhaps because his situation was so new to him, because so many years had passed since his last love affair, he found himself strutting like a boy just launched upon his first. If he had the nerve, he thought, he would go by way of Jimmy's house to ask if he had returned home; but the impulse to reach Nélida's as soon as possible was stronger. It was as if with her beside him he would be safe, not from the young people—this threat had almost ceased to alarm him—but from contagion to which he was clearly susceptible (given the sensitivity he felt for his environment), the insidious and terrible contagion of old age.

XXXIII

PERHAPS because the morning was cold and damp he did not meet a single "repression squad" along the way. *Real terrors,* he thought, *but evidently they're not taking any chances with their health.* At Plaza Güemes he recalled that this was where he had flagged down the taxi on his way back from the cemetery. It seemed incredible that all that had happened, not in some remote past, but only a day before. Sheltered by the great trees with their delicate green foliage arching over his head, he walked along Guatemala, looking for house numbers and taking care to stay out of sight of a gang of young people gathered at the corner ahead. The number he was looking for—4174—turned out to be a building consisting of two separate structures; between them lay a small garden, with a magnolia tree and a sun-dial. He opened the front door, which was ajar, stepped inside, referred to his piece of paper, then opened another door with the larger key. Without encountering a soul in the hall, he went up the stairs, opened a third door and went down a long corridor. On the left, beyond a balustrade, was a patio; on the right a series of doors. A young woman was standing in the second or third doorway. She eyed him boldly, and he thought, *Poor Nélida, she talked so much about the house she was going to have, and she's moved into just another miserable tenement.* Again he checked the directions she had given him, went up a little wrought-iron spiral staircase, and found himself facing a door with the number five on a round plaque of white enamel. He knocked, not wanting to barge in, and was just about to insert the key in the lock when Nélida opened the door.

"What a relief!" she cried. "I was afraid you might have second thoughts and not come after all. Come in. Now I know nothing can go wrong for us."

He thought wonderingly, *Most women are unwilling to show their love. They play safe. They haven't the self-confidence she has, or the strength.*

The apartment took his breath away. *A really impressive place. She wasn't exaggerating.* The main room, which seemed enormous, with its high plaster ceiling ornamented with garlands, had actually been converted into two rooms: at one end a dining-area with table and chairs, buffet and refrigerator; at the other a sitting-room with a table, a wicker sofa, armchairs, a rocker, and a television set. He could see part of the bed and the wardrobe in the adjoining room. After so many doors, stairs, and passageways, he was all the more surprised to find himself in such a well-furnished and comfortable apartment.

"It's good to be here."

"You didn't bring much with you."

"You yourself suggested I should try to conceal the move."

"Are you going to stay?"

"If you'll have me."

"We'll wait for a few days, and when things calm down a bit we'll go get your things. Will you excuse me a minute? I'm getting dinner ready."

While she was busy in the kitchen, he wandered around. There was an inner court with flowering plants and a bedroom with a double bed, a wardrobe, and two night tables. On the wall, in heavy oval mahogany frames, hung two photographs, rather like pen-and-ink sketches, of a man and a woman of some bygone time.

"Who are the people in the photographs?"

"My grandparents," she called out from the kitchen. "Don't

worry, I'll take them down. I just didn't feel right about doing it the first thing after I'd moved in."

He was about to reply that they did not bother him in the least, but he stopped himself: it might be a tactless thing to say. He felt comfortable in this house. Too bad he had not brought all his things with him: it was mortifying to think of having to go back to Paunero Street, however briefly. In the midst of his sense of well being, one disturbing thought came to him: *Can I live here without feeling like a kept man?*

XXXIV

One thing surprised him: Nélida had not tried to conceal from him her eagerness to make love. *It surprises me that I'm surprised,* he thought. *I wasn't born yesterday, and I should know by this time that . . .* He no doubt felt that the girl had made him a gift. Lying beside her, stretched out on his back, relaxed and at peace, he fell to wondering idly about the statement he had heard so many times, that everyone is sad after making love. He recalled, too, how his friends had spoken of their hurry to get away, to be out-of-doors, to be home again. He could only conclude that few men, as a rule, were as fortunate as he was. He rolled over and looked at her, wanting to express his gratitude in words.

"You're sure you won't miss your old house?" she asked.

"Of course not!"

"People get used to familiar things."

"For instance the having to cross the open courtyard to go to the bathroom? If you're used to it, it's not too hard to keep on that way; but after just one day of living in pleasant surroundings, it's unthinkable to go back."

"I know now I could never go back and live with *doña* Dalmacia and her granddaughters. It's odd you never thought of moving yourself."

"There was one time when I had a little money and I was going to move. My wife had left me, I was all alone with the boy; but thanks to the neighbors, who took care of him when I wasn't around, I was able to go on working. Everything has its compensations . . ."

It seemed to him that as he spoke Nélida looked more and more preoccupied. *Am I boring her?* he wondered in alarm. *She's young, she's used to young friends, and for years now it seems I've talked only to old people.*

"And so you didn't buy the apartment?"

"You didn't buy them in those days, you rented them. No, that dream never came true. Like the dream I had of becoming a teacher. There was a time once when I wanted to be a teacher. Hard to believe, isn't it?"

She seemed somehow pleased to consider his having entertained such an ambition. As they exchanged reminiscences, he noted that when she spoke of something that happened two or three years before, Nélida would invariably say "long ago." Suddenly he thought again of the conversation she was going to have with her fiancé, which deeply concerned him. "Have you told your fiancé yet?"

"Not yet. I'll have to talk to him."

He would have given a great deal to have that moment over and done with. "I'll go with you, if you'd like me to."

"Oh, no, that won't be necessary. Martín's not a bad sort."

"Martín who?"

"My fiancé. I wouldn't feel right saying what I have to unless we were alone."

"Where will you see him?"

"That depends. Up until five he's at the garage. After that I'd have to look for him wherever he happens to be working. Did I tell you he plays in a trio called *Los Porteñitos?*

"Yes, you did. Better see him at the garage. I don't like to think of your wandering around cafes, especially at night."

"He plays in The Corner Spot, on Thames Street, and in a basement, in a little cabaret called FOB, and in the Salon Maguenta in Plaza Güemes. I'll be right back, I have to go into the kitchen a minute. Aren't you hungry?"

He stayed in bed, on his back, too tired to go with her, or even to change his position. *But this is a different kind of tiredness, there's nothing depressing about it. It's comforting. A little bit like a diploma on the wall.* Too bad the conversation with her ex-fiancé was still pending. He had nothing against the fellow, but it was regrettable that on his account Nélida should have to go to The Corner Spot or the Salon Maguenta, to say nothing of that basement place with the peculiar name. To take his mind off the subject, he started thinking about the apartment he had come close to renting: he would have lived in the Once neighborhood, he would have had different friends (except for Jimmy, whom he had known since school), and he would not have met Nélida. In this room, with her beside him, it seemed impossible that people were shooting each other in the streets of Buenos Aires . . . Letting his imagination run on, he thought how strange it would be if the war were confined to the area around Plaza Las Heras, and was all the plot of a single bully named Bogliolo, designed for a single victim, Isidro Vidal.

"Come to dinner," Nélida called.

There was a platter of ravioli on the table.

"I'm starved."

"I don't know if you'll like them."

He set her mind at rest: ravioli brought back memories of happy times, of Sundays in his childhood, of his mother. "Believe me," he told her, with genuine enthusiasm, "these are even better than I'd remembered. And I thought I'd never taste anything that good again."

They had red wine, breaded veal chops, and fried potatoes. When she brought the rice pudding, she said, "If you don't like it, please say so. I don't know yet what your favorite dishes are."

He kissed her for that "yet," which seemed to promise a long life together. Then he fell silent: what could he add, what more could he say, without running the risk of boring her? He drank another glass of wine, and when she got up to put the coffee on, he began to kiss her again.

XXXV

He stretched out his hand confidently toward the girl, and did not find her. The displeasure wakened him with a start; he looked to his left, she was not there. With a terrible sense of foreboding, he leaped out of bed, went through the other rooms, then flung open the door on to the patio.

"Nélida! Nélida!" he called.

The girl had disappeared. Filled with anxiety—though he had probably no cause—he tried to understand. Suddenly it all came back, he remembered perfectly how Nélida had bent over him and spoken. One by one the words came back. "I'm going to settle things with Martín. Don't leave, and don't open the door to anyone. Wait for me, I won't be long."

Although he was almost asleep, he had understood the words perfectly. He had been distressed and irritated (the idea of her referring to him by his first name!), but as if held down by a dead weight of weariness—the endless nights without sleep, the journey back from the cemetery, the night in the attic, the ardent lovemaking—he had simply lain there, incapable of objecting, incapable of moving. *Like an idiot, I let her go. And here I am, shut up in a cage.* She had said (in the tone of a doctor trying to reassure a patient), "I won't be long"; but since he did not know when she had gone, he should not reject the possibility that it had been only a few minutes earlier, and that, for all her good intentions, she might be delayed until Lord knows when. With deliberate slowness, he got dressed. To pass the time, he went into the kitchen to make some *maté*. Searching for matches and the kettle, he wondered if the future really held a life for him with Nélida, there in that house. Very carefully he steeped the first *maté* and drank it; then, in rapid sequence, four or five more. It occurred to him that it had been some time since he had checked to see if there was any news about Jimmy. He found it continually hard to go on waiting for Nélida. He was sure she would never return, particularly if he couldn't take his mind off her. He had already resorted to *maté;* and now he lacked the patience either to wait or to think of something else to do. Clearly, if he went to Jimmy's it would take his mind off waiting, and, with any luck at all, he would find Nélida there when he got back. However, he thought it better to let a few more minutes pass, to give her a chance to get back. If she came in before he had left, this would avoid a number of risks which he preferred not to think about. But the truth is that much of the time a person does not do what he chooses, but what he is able to. And what he was unable to do was stay here, ruminating aimlessly.

He threw on his poncho, switched off the light, groped for the latch, stepped out on to the landing, and locked the door. Slowly he went down the iron stairway. *Time's up. I'm going out.* Although he wanted to turn back, he continued along the narrow corridor. *People here don't hide their curiosity,* he thought, noting how they were watching him as he passed their doorways. *Why didn't I leave a note to say I was going to Jimmy's and would be right back?* And with a flash of resentment, *That will teach her.* Was it genuine, this outburst of jealousy, or was it merely an excuse not to go back to that empty apartment he had been waiting in? He must not let his nerves run away with him, as if he were some hysterical woman. Jimmy used to say that all troubles came from not knowing how to control one's nerves. To control his own, Vidal began walking very slowly. *I'm giving her one last chance to return, and she's passing it up, out of sheer stubbornness.* At the street door he hesitated a while, looking this way and that, intent less on the ambush that might be waiting in the shadows of the trees than on the impossible chance that Nélida might suddenly appear. Wouldn't the quickest way out of this stupid anxiety perhaps be to go look for her in one of those cafes where this Martín fellow was playing? However, he could not overlook a disagreeable possibility—that she would be annoyed with him for coming, think of him, suddenly, as a man incapable of controlling himself or of trusting her. And he would begin then to lose her love, a misfortune that was inevitable in any case: absurd to suppose that such a pretty young girl could love him. His ill-timed arrival would disillusion her. She would realize her mistake, be cured of her caprice. She might even tell him then and there to clear out, that she was staying with Martín. (Ever since he first heard the name, he had detested it.) He pictured himself retreating in disgrace, amid the jeers of the crowd, while at the back of the room the happy pair fell into each other's arms: the closing scenes of a movie, with the villain punished (the old man), and the young lovers together at last, the music swelling triumphantly and the audience applauding.

By way of Salguero he came into Plaza Güemes. *What is this mania I have for always taking the same streets? This must be just about where Guadalupe Lake used to be.* Between Arenales and Juncal he asked himself, *Have I forgotten Nélida?* Up to then he had been trying to do exactly that, feeling somehow, that his very expectancy was preventing her return. Now, forgetting her seemed like forsaking her. *I wonder if anything has happened to her . . . This is where the penitentiary used to be.* The disconnected nature of his thoughts was a sure sign he was growing desperate. He had a sudden urge to talk to Dante, who lived nearby, on French Street. *Admittedly, poor Dante is not very entertaining.* After the events of the last few days, it was affection rather than habit that bound each one to the others of the group. True, he would look at them sometimes with apprehension, or something close to it, as if they were addicted to a vice, the vice of old age, from which Nélida's love would preserve him. The tactics of superstition. That way some hope would remain of getting her back again. Whereas if he were too confident, he would be punished for his presumption by never seeing her again. *Instead,* he thought with resignation, *I'll go see Dante.*

Dante lived in the only one-story house still standing on the block, a squat sort of mausoleum between two tall buildings. But it was not Dante whom he saw first: it was "the *señora*" who answered the door. This was the way Dante always referred to her; nobody knew for certain whether she was his housekeeper or his wife. Very likely she was both. Clad in loose black garments, she peered at him like a frightened animal, with the distrust that the sight of a young person now aroused in older people. *Apparently,* he thought, *there are some people who don't take me for an old man.* Her reddish skin was covered with dark hairs; her hair was black too, streaked with gray. Age had doubtless coarsened her features, as it so often does: they were thickened and prominent. Had this hag ever been—was she still, perhaps—Dante's bedmate? Unimaginable things go on behind bedroom doors. *The idea is so repulsive you can't help wishing them both an early death. Granted, if I should happen to live to that age myself, and still felt the urge, I wouldn't be so finicky as to turn some woman down. By that time any indication at all that I'm still alive would be precious.*

The woman was about to close the door in his face. "I'm Isidoro Vidal," he cried out. "Tell *señor* Dante that Isidoro is here."

Nudging the woman to one side, Dante appeared on the threshold. "Here I am." He was smiling complacently.

His color was bad, a waxen pallor, tinged with green. Did he seem even older, Vidal wondered, in contrast to Nélida's youth? "How are you?" he asked.

"Fine. First of all, I've got some good news for you. Jimmy's back."

"Really?"

"Rey told me. He phoned less than half an hour ago."

"In good shape?"

"I'm fine. Just like a kid. I've never felt better."

"I meant is Jimmy all right? Shall we go see him?"

"Rey told me not to go without stopping by the bakery. He has something to tell me. Serious enough so that he wants to tell me it in person. With all these terrible things going on, I didn't have the nerve to go out by myself. If you want to, let's go together."

"Let's go to Jimmy's instead."

"No. Rey very particularly asked me not to without stopping by the bakery first."

"The trouble is, I haven't much time, and I want very much to see Jimmy."

"I want to get back home in a hurry too. Half blind and half deaf the way I am, I'd be an easy prey at night. I'm in no hurry to die, believe me. Just so long as you understand I have to get back from Rey's as soon as I can."

XXXVI

SEATED at the head of the table, with a daughter at each side and a third facing him, Leandro Rey was finishing dinner. He invited his friends to join him. Vidal accepted a cup of coffee; Dante wanted nothing. Coffee kept him awake, and alcohol in any form gave him an acid stomach.

"Have they released Jimmy?" Vidal asked.

"Yes—but just a minute." In a tone of authority, Rey addressed his daughters: "Clear the table and leave us alone. We have important things to discuss."

His daughters looked back angrily at him, but they obeyed.

"Holy smoke!" Dante exclaimed, when they were alone. "And all the time I thought it was your girls who gave the orders around here."

"I used to let them have their own way before, but now they watch their step. I'd be in trouble if they didn't."

"In the present circumstances," suggested Dante, "wouldn't it be more prudent to follow a policy of, say, appeasement?"

Rey's only reply was an indignant snort.

Vidal asked again, "Then they've released Jimmy?"

"He came home this morning."

"Let's go see him."

"Not right now. At least I'm not going."

"Why not?"

"Well, I have my reasons. There's an ugly rumor going around, and I mean ugly."

"What can he have done that you don't want to see him? Anyway, what does it matter? Jimmy's our friend."

"So is Arévalo," said Rey solemnly. "Or was."

"Just what has happened?"

"It seems that, to obtain his release, Jimmy turned informer: he told them Arévalo was having an affair with a teen-aged girl, and let them know just when and where to find them. Now Jimmy's at home, and Arévalo is in Fernández Hospital. That's the story."

"How did you hear all this?"

"Before dinner, just about closing time, Faber showed up at the bakery. He'd just been talking to Bogliolo, whose nephew had told him the story, complete with details."

"And then?"

"That's all. If you come that late, the bread's all gone. I told him I had nothing left but Melba toast."

"But what happened to Arévalo?"

"He's been going with that girl a long time," said Dante.

Vidal stared at him. "I'm always the last one to find out. But I had noticed he was looking more presentable lately—elegant, almost. Not even his dandruff showed."

"A gang of ruffians was waiting for him when they came out of the Hotel Nile," said Rey. "The girl started screaming at the top of her lungs: 'I like old men! I like them.' "

"Egging them on. I'd like to gun her down," said Dante savagely. "She's the one who's responsible."

"She's not," said Vidal.

"Dante, don't talk nonsense. Here at last is an honest girl, ready to die for her convictions, and all you can do is growl at her."

"My hat's off to her," said Vidal. "What did they do to Arévalo?"

"They left him for dead. I suggest we go by the hospital and try to find out how he's getting along."

"The girl's just a dirty little rabble-rouser," muttered Dante.

"I haven't got all the time in the world," said Vidal. "What do you say we get going right now."

The words were no sooner out of his mouth than he was conscious of how thoughtless they must sound. For him, naturally, nothing mattered so much as his relationship with Nélida, but how, at this moment, could he even speak of it? Rey and Dante might congratulate him, envy his good fortune, but they would certainly disapprove of his taking it seriously, or valuing it above a lifelong friendship.

"You can drop me off at my place," said Dante. "I really prefer to go home. I've no desire to be out on the street at night in times like these, believe me."

XXXVII

TALKING animatedly, Vidal and Rey headed out the door of the shop and turned left along Salguero. Dante regarded them sadly, like a child on the verge of tears. Overtaking them, he grabbed Rey's arm. "Why don't you take me home?"

"Let go," said Rey, shaking him off. In a matter-of-fact voice he explained, "We're going to find out about Arévalo."

"Don't speak so loudly, please. You'll draw attention," said Dante.

"I may have been born in Spain," Rey went on, "but this is my city."

"So what?" Dante asked.

"What do you mean, so what? I've lived in Buenos Aires longer than these young toughs, and they're not going to take what's mine away from me."

"Fine," said Vidal. "It's fine for you to stand your ground. But look, are you sure you aren't jumping to conclusions? I'm not about to have a falling out with Jimmy on account of some gossip Bogliolo's spread around!"

"Listen, when I hear the word *informer,* I see red."

Vidal spoke earnestly. "How can you be sure it's not just some new trick? That Bogliolo's nephew isn't attempting to divide us and turn us against each other?"

"Psychological warfare," said Dante.

"Well—there may be a grain of truth in what Dante says,"

admitted Rey grudgingly. "But in any case, I could never forgive an informer."

"But could you think that Jimmy would give a friend away on the strength of an empty promise?"

"Empty promise?"

"They could have gotten to Arévalo without releasing Jimmy."

"Jimmy's capable of anything."

Dante glanced back fearfully. "The thing that alarms me is that the city looks perfectly normal, as if nothing was happening at all."

"Maybe a little street brawl would make you feel more comfortable," Vidal suggested.

"We had one yesterday," Rey said. "Right nearby, in front of Vilaseco's hotel. Some juvenile delinquents from the Youth Guild tried to take the place by assault. But Vilaseco, with the help of his loyal employee Paco, held off the attack. When all seemed lost, they came on with bare fists, and saved the place."

XXXVIII

The three friends went up the steps and into the lobby of Fernández Hospital. In the half-light they noticed something that, from a distance, appeared to be a statue covered by a sheet. Rey went up closer to get a good look.

"What is it?" Dante asked.

"An old man."

"An old man?"

"Yes, an old man on a stretcher."

"What is he doing?" Dante asked, keeping his distance.

"I think he's dying."

"Why did we have to come here?" Dante moaned.

"We'll all end up in one hospital or another," said Rey amiably. "Why not get used to it?"

"But I'm tired. You two don't realize. I feel very old. Néstor's death, and the pointless attack on us in the cemetery, and now this business with Arévalo. It's all made me sick. I just don't have the heart to keep up the struggle."

They came to a room which was separated from the lobby by a half-partition and a small window. "We'd like to get some information about a gentleman who was admitted last night," Rey told the attendant. "The name is Arévalo."

"When did he come in?"

"I don't like the looks of this place," said Dante loudly.

Poor devil, Vidal thought. *If I told him we were leaving him here, he'd burst out crying.*

"He was brought in last night," said Rey.

"To what ward?"

"That's just what we don't know," said Vidal. "He had been beaten."

Dante, meanwhile, had been rubbing his gums and then sniffing his finger. "What's wrong with you?" Vidal asked him.

"It works loose, and food particles get lodged inside, and it begins to stink," Dante explained. "You have a denture too. You'll see."

"Are you all related to the injured man?" asked a short man with a round head that resembled a halloween pumpkin. On the upper left-hand pocket of his white coat *Doctor L. Cadelago* was stitched in blue thread.

"No, we're not relatives," Vidal answered. "We're friends. Close friends."

"It makes no difference," said the doctor quickly. "Come on, let's go."

"Tell me, doctor," said Rey, "how is he?"

The doctor stopped short, seemingly immersed in his own thoughts. Then he appeared disturbed by the question. With an anxiety he could not conceal, Dante asked: "Nothing bad has happened to him?"

The doctor's face clouded. "Nothing bad? I don't understand, what do you mean by that?"

"Our friend Arévalo—he's not dead, is he?" Dante stammered out.

"No," replied the doctor gravely.

"Is his condition critical?" murmured Vidal.

The doctor smiled. Arévalo's friends expectantly awaited a word of reassurance. "Yes it is. It's touch and go right now."

"How awful!" exclaimed Vidal.

Doctor Cadelago's expression once more grew sad. "Today we have ways of dealing with this kind of condition."

"But do you think, Doctor, that he'll pull through?" Vidal asked.

"No medical man with a sense of his professional responsibility would answer such a question." In an ominous tone he continued, "The means exist to cope with this kind of situation. There's no question of that, we have the means."

Suddenly Vidal had a feeling he had met Doctor Cadelago before, or someone else who invariably smiled when he was most disturbed—or perhaps it was only in his dreams that he had met this person . . . They fell in line behind the doctor, who appeared to be crushed by the weight of his responsibilities, and followed him to the elevator. "This guy doesn't make any sense," Vidal whispered to Rey.

"How could he, when we know nothing about medicine? You have to realize that we live in a different world."

"Fortunately." *We go through life feeling secure,* Vidal thought, *and even in the midst of the war we still think that accidents happen only to other people; but if a friend dies—or we're told that he may die—everything becomes unreal . . .* Things took on a different light now—the way they do in a theatre when the technician slides a filter of a different color in front of the projector. The doctor, with the expression that seemed perpetually at odds with the words that issued from his mouth, and that curious head—like a hollow pumpkin that you put a candle in to scare children at night—seemed himself a creature out of some fantasy. Vidal felt he had walked into a nightmare, or rather, that he was living in a nightmare. *But Nélida exists,* he thought, feeling a current of strength run through him. *But does she exist for me?*

Dante, still cringing, uttered a feeble protest. "How much longer are we going to stay here? I don't like being in this place. Why don't we leave right now?"

He's an old man, thought Vidal, *no denying it.* The process of aging had speeded up, and there was barely a trace left of the friend they had known: of late he had turned into something else, someone disagreeable whom they continued to see only out of a loyalty to the past.

As they entered the elevator, the doctor asked, "You're all past sixty?"

"I'm not," answered Vidal promptly.

They got off at the fifth floor. *So far as not liking this place goes,* he thought, *I'm with Dante. If you consider the freedom outside these walls, it makes you feel afraid, as though you might have left it behind forever.*

XXXIX

"HERE is his room," said the doctor.

Along both sides of the corridor ran a series of little rooms, some with two beds, some with four, divided by white partitions. Arévalo lifted his hand as they came in. *That's a good sign,* Vidal thought, and then he noticed the broad welts running across Arévalo's face. The bed next to his was empty.

"What happened?" asked Rey.

"I'm going to make my rounds," said the doctor. "Don't get him excited. It's all right to talk, but don't get him excited."

"I had a little mishap, Rey. They beat me up."

There were two bruises on his face: a deep gash running beneath one cheekbone, and a broader purplish streak across the forehead.

"How are you feeling?" Vidal asked.

"A bit sore. Not just in the face, in the kidneys. They kicked me while I was on the ground; the doctor says it caused an internal hemorrhage. He gave me these pills to take."

The bottle was on the night-table, beside a glass of water and a small clock. The clock seemed to Vidal to be ticking very fast; he thought of Nélida, and the impatient sweep of the second hand seemed to him to be in some way linked to the girl he missed. He felt suddenly dejected.

"Why did they do it?" asked Rey.

"It was all planned. They were waiting for me. At first they were hesitant, then they rushed at me."

"Like yapping dogs," said Vidal.

Arévalo smiled.

"If it hadn't been for that girl's words, maybe they wouldn't have beaten you up," said Dante. "We all know what women are like: they enjoy stirring things up. They're eternal troublemakers."

"Let's not exaggerate," said Arévalo.

"Dante reminds me of those old men who develop a hatred for the opposite sex," said Vidal. "And the younger the female, the more contempt they have."

"The way I see it," said Rey, "there's no reason to lay the blame on women. It's the young people who are to blame."

"But they have their virtues," said Arévalo. "For one thing, they're disinterested. It may be because they haven't had much experience, or simply that they haven't had time to acquire the taste for money."

"Perhaps money seems unimportant because it's something they expect to have later," suggested Vidal.

"While for old people," said Arévalo, "it develops into their single passion."

"Single passion?" echoed Vidal. "What about gluttony, and selfishness, and obsessions of all kinds? Haven't you seen how greedily they cling to the little scrap of life that's left to them? The terrified expression on their faces when they have to cross the street?"

"It's not that I condemn youth as a whole," said Rey. "Show me a pretty girl and I'll gobble her up on the spot. But if a bunch of young ruffians want to take me on, they'll get a real fight."

"That's fine, if you can handle them. The most I could do was to shield my face and head—and at that I came off better than the man in the next bed."

"The bed's empty," Dante pointed out.

"Even though he never stopped talking, I don't think he recovered consciousness. He started ranting about his dreams. He dreamed that he was young again and back with his friends in the Pedigree Cafe on the corner of Santa Fe and Serrano, discussing tango lyrics. He even mentioned a fellow named Tronget who was an authority on country themes . . ."

"You were listening pretty closely," Dante remarked.

"Do you suppose he was a songwriter himself?" asked Vidal.

"That's what I gathered. I don't know how many times he mentioned a tango called *El Cosquilloso,* which seems to have been one of his greatest successes. He said the same thing twenty times over."

"*El Cosquilloso?* Nobody remembers that old ditty any more," said Dante.

"He talked about how he missed the conversations he used to have, when he and his friends would sit up till all hours arguing about the proper way to set words to a tango, or discussing the twists and turns of the plot in Ivo Pelay's latest comedy. Today, he said, all people can talk about is facts, and mostly about how much everything costs. His mind seemed pretty clear at that point, but then he began to wander again. When his breathing started getting irregular they took him away."

"Where?" asked Dante.

"To die alone," answered Rey.

"They do that," Arévalo explained, "so as not to undermine the morale of the poor fellow in the next bed."

"That cafe where they used to meet could have been like ours in the Plaza Las Heras," said Vidal, as though talking to himself.

"You can't compare the two," said Arévalo, "The atmosphere there was something quite different."

"When are we going to get back to playing cards?" Vidal asked.

"Pretty soon now," said Arévalo. "The doctor thinks so anyway. He says we're witnessing the last stages of the uprising.

"What if we don't survive until it's finished?" asked Vidal.

"That's possible. Clearly they've got us all marked. In my case, at least, I'm convinced it was all planned. At first they hesitated, and then they came at me."

"Either he's repeating himself, or I'm not hearing properly," said Dante.

"Tell me," asked Vidal, "what happened to the man in the other bed?"

"Like you, he went to the funeral service of a friend. When he left to head home, they grabbed him outside the funeral parlor."

"I want to go," Dante whimpered. "Rey, please, come with me. I feel old, very old. Just the thought of an attack terrifies me."

His face had been pallid before; now it was ashen. *Don't go to pieces here,* thought Vidal.

"The employees at the funeral parlor were all for carrying him inside, but a policeman showed up and brought him here."

"It would have been more practical to leave him at the undertakers," Rey commented.

"You said that they took him away to die by himself. Where?" Dante asked.

"Oh, I don't know where they take them. One of the male nurses told me they set them down just anywhere. Since he's fairly young, he probably thinks of me as an old man he can throw a scare into by painting grisly pictures. He said they put them anywhere, even right in the middle of the lobby."

"Poor guy," said Vidal. "If he's still alive what do you suppose he's dreaming about now?"

"He's the one we saw when we came in," Dante wailed. "Rey, I want to go home."

"Actually, I was about to leave," said Rey. "I have to be up early to supervise the baking; and if I don't get my eight hours of sleep, I'm no good for anything."

"You'll drop me at my house on your way, won't you?" Dante begged.

Nélida is waiting for me, thought Vidal, *and here I stay. Nobody's waiting for these two, but they can't stay a minute longer with a sick friend. One of them is a slave to his egotism, and the other to his cowardice. There's nothing worse than old age.* He immediately had a second thought: *Perhaps the fact that I'm here with Arévalo, that I haven't gone back to the apartment, means that I'm old too. But I know that I'm staying deliberately to give her time, so that I won't get back ahead of her. To return and not find her there would be horrible.*

The doctor came back in. "Please, gentlemen, don't go just yet. I'd like to keep you a few minutes longer, at least the youngest of you. It's a little blood sample, just in case we have to give the patient a transfusion. It doesn't amount to anything, you know, just a little prick of the needle."

He switched on a lamp and began to tap Arévalo's chest. Looking across at Dante, over the doctor's bald head, Arévalo remarked, "Your hair's showing white at the roots, Dante. You'll have to touch it up."

The doctor scratched his head nervously. "If you talk when I have my head up against your chest," he explained, "it tickles me."

"I didn't understand what you said," Dante told Arévalo. "When you swallow your words that way, I can't understand you."

"It's my asthma. I was saying your hair's showing white at the roots."

"What do you expect? It's not the sort of thing you notice yourself. Besides, who'll do it for me? Poor Néstor dyed it the last time. I can't do it alone. It's really very important, you know."

"It doesn't fool anyone," said Arévalo. "If you ask me, you have to be a bit of a fatalist."

"That's easy to say if you're holed up in a building like this, which is practically a fortress. But I have to make it home in the dark, through streets that are completely unlit."

"Nobody's throwing you out," Vidal told him.

"I'll be right back, gentlemen," said the doctor. "Please wait for me."

"Let's go before he comes," Dante begged. "Isidro's stuck here now. He can't get out of the transfusion. They don't need us.

We don't have to stay and hold Arévalo's hand. If we do, they'll think up some way to trap us. Let's get away before he comes back. I don't like being here."

"You're not alone in that," Arévalo told him.

"I don't believe they want to trap us," said Rey. "But it's late, I have to get up early, and our being here serves no purpose. Isidro has to stay, of course."

"Of course," said Vidal. "Go ahead. We don't need you."

Rey opened his mouth, but said nothing. Dante, like a stubborn child, was tugging at his sleeve and pushing him towards the door.

"Have they gone?" Arévalo asked.

"They're gone."

"Were you angry?"

"A little upset with them both."

"Don't be angry. Remember what Jimmy always says: in time the control mechanism breaks down. Dante can no more help being afraid than some one else can help wetting the bed."

"Dante's given up. But Rey. That fine fellow . . ."

"But he lost control long ago. You've watched him at the cafe, fairly quivering with gluttony, wolfing down olives. No sense of shame—like so many old people."

"Shameless? You're right there. One day at Vilaseco's . . ."

"Age has turned him into a bare-faced egotist. He doesn't even try to hide it. He cares about his own comfort, and that's the end of it."

XL

"WILL you kindly come this way?" asked Dr. Cadelago.

Following him along the corridor, Vidal said, "Arévalo was telling me, doctor, that you believe this war is just about over."

"Believe me," replied the doctor, shaking his head sadly, "our psychiatric service is inadequate to meet the needs of the young people. They all come with the same problem: they're terrified at the thought of contact with the old. It amounts to a positive repulsion."

"Repulsion? That seems natural enough to me."

"It's stronger than they are. This is something new, and it's established beyond question: the young are identifying with the old. In the course of this war they've come to understand that every old man is what one young man or another will someday become. Age is their own future. And another curious thing: invariably you find them constructing the same fantasy, that killing an old man is kind of suicide."

"Don't you think it's more likely that the misery and the ugliness of the victim makes the crime more painful to commit?"

Why do I bother with this, Vidal wondered. *Why do I go on talking to this idiot, when the only thing that matters is the girl who's waiting for me?*

"Every normal child," explained the doctor gleefully, "goes through a stage of eviscerating cats. I did myself. Later on we blot out the memory of these childish games, we eliminate them, we excrete them. This present war will pass and leave no memories behind."

They came to a cubicle. Vidal thought: *Just to keep from annoying this stuffed shirt, I'm making Nélida wait and worry about me.* No, he wasn't being fair to himself. He was there, not because he was afraid of annoying anyone, but because he thought he might possibly be of help to Arévalo. Or had he really come because Rey had made a point of it, and was he giving blood now because the doctor had asked him to? As Isidorito's lady psychiatrist kept proving, there were an infinite number of explanations for everything.

"Afterwards may I go, doctor?"

"I can't see any reason why not. It won't take long. Just lie down quietly for a few minutes on this cot, and make yourself comfortable. There's no hurry."

"Somebody's waiting for me, doctor."

"Congratulations. Not all of us can say as much."

"Just how long will it take?"

"Women and children can't help being impatient, but we men have schooled ourselves to it. Even though there may be nothing for us at the end of it all we still wait."

"Christ," said Vidal.

"There now," said the doctor. "Just a little jab of the needle. Now don't move your arm. Afterwards get yourself a cup of coffee and a glass of fruit juice, and you'll be as good as new. It's essential to replace the fluids."

Nélida is surely back in the apartment by now, Vidal thought. *But suppose she hasn't come home yet?* He rejected the notion at once; it was intolerable.

"Finished?" he asked.

"Now I want you to close your eyes for me, and wait here until I come back."

Why didn't he tell the idiot to go to hell, and walk out? Weary and dispirited, he felt incapable of saying a firm "no" to these little delays which kept turning up one after another, each one promising to be the very last, surely taking no more than a minute of his time. In this fashion, the visit to the hospital had dragged on, had become a nightmare providing subtle and inexhaustible sources of anxiety. It is apparent that he must have fallen asleep at last, for he seemed to see assembled on a high platform a group of young men, among whom he recognized the killers of the newspaper vendor. They formed some sort of menacing tribunal from which they were calling down to him.

"What's going on?" he asked.

"Nothing," said Dr. Cadelago, in a distressed tone. "You're free to go."

He went back to say goodbye to Arévalo.

XLI

He had supposed that once he was outside and headed toward Guatemala Street, he would feel elated. In his impatience he had confused this moment with that other one, more distant in time and much more eagerly longed for, when he would rejoin Nélida. No sooner had he left the hospital than it struck him that that reunion, while surely possible, was by no means certain. He realized too that he felt depressed. Perhaps becoming depressed beforehand was his way of preparing himself for a disappointment.

At Salguero he turned left in the direction of Plaza Las Heras. Why should he tie Nélida down to a dying animal? Neither of them had anything to gain. All she could look forward to was disillusionment, which he could foresee but not forestall . . . the behavior of Rey and Dante had made him sick at the thought of old age. His feeling for these friends was no longer the same. *Everything changes with time. And people more than anything else.* He recalled, in vivid flashes which quickly faded, a scene in which a prosecutor, insane with rage, had accused him of being an old man. The memory which came from the dream he had had right after the transfusion now had a profoundly saddening effect. Far from being a new man, he felt lifeless and dispirited; and the fruit juice which the doctor had prescribed would not help this dejection. To be old was to be condemned beyond hope of pardon, and without hope, desire and ambition were unthinkable. How could he possibly delude himself into making plans which, even if he could carry them out, would avail him nothing, or virtually nothing? What was the poit of going to Guatemala Street now? Better just to go home. Unfortunately, Nélida would come looking for him, asking for an explanation. Young people cannot understand how having no future to look forward to eliminates everything that is important in life to an old person. *The sickness is not the sick person,* he thought, *but an old man is old age, and there is no other way out but death.* Unexpectedly, the realization that he was totally without hope put new life into him. He hastened his steps, so as to reach Nélida's sooner, to be there before this conviction faded, as the memory of his dream had faded. For the very reason that he loved her so, he must convince her that her love for an old man like him was an illusion.

He heard an explosion, perhaps of a bomb that had burst somewhere not far off. Then he heard two more detonations. From somewhere near the vicinity of Retiro Station, a redness appeared that rapidly began to spread up and out across the sky.

XLII

He switched on the light, glanced around, looked into the bedroom, then hurriedly glanced through the rest of the apartment. Probably it was all a game: the moment his back was turned Nélida would pop up from somewhere and throw her arms around him. But he quickly realized that he must face the possibility—or rather the probability, as the minutes went by—that she had not returned. It was not, he told himself, an especially dramatic situation; he felt sure that one day, very soon perhaps, he would no longer recall this moment of anguish (if things worked out for the two of them). But right now, for reasons that he accepted without understanding, he could not endure it. He said aloud, *I'm not going to abandon her to that dance-hall musician.*

He left the apartment, and walked north along Güemes determined to find Nélida, to get her back again. The despondency he had felt such a short while before had disappeared; he had no sense of weariness, or defeat, or old age.

Seeing a cab, he raised his hand and flagged it down boldly. He got in and ordered the driver, "Take me to Thames Street. I'm going to a place called the Salon Maguenta. Do you know it?"

The car jerked forward and sped off, throwing him against the rear seat. "Yes, sir, it's a night club. Good idea. People have to get out and have themselves a little bit of fun, now that the war's nearly over."

"You think so?" At the same moment Vidal asked himself, *Why didn't I notice? He's young.* Suddenly he pictured himself being dumped out at San Petrito cemetery, picking himself up, a mass of bruises after his fall from the cab. He nearly voiced his thought: *If I have to start from there, it will set me back hours* . . . In a detached fashion he said, "It's been almost over for quite some time now," and irritated by his own tone of acceptance, he went on: "I lost a friend in this, a life-long friend. There weren't many like him. I wish someone would explain to me what the world and his murderers gained by his death."

When he saw they were driving now along Güemes toward the Pacific Railway station, he told himself there was nothing to fear.

"I understand how you must feel, sir, but with all due respect, I don't think you're looking at it in the right light."

"What do you mean?"

"I mean that if people stopped to weigh the gains against the losses—the destruction and the suffering—we'd never have wars or revolutions."

"But since we're men of iron, the suffering doesn't matter," replied Vidal. *He must be a student,* he thought, *working to put himself through school.* "I'll go further than that. I don't believe there can be any positive side to this war."

"I agree with you."

"Well, then?"

"You can't judge it by the results. It's a protest."

"I ask you, what had my friend Néstor done?"

"Nothing at all, sir. Neither you nor I like what's been happening. Put the responsibility where it belongs."

"Where is that?"

"On the people who made the world what it is."

"What does that have to do with the old people?"

"They represent the past. The young can't go out and kill our great national heroes, the men who have made history, for the very good reason that they're already dead."

By the way that the young man stressed the word *dead,* Vidal could sense the hostility. *But I'm not going to reject his reasoning, simply because he's my enemy.* He was exasperated with himself: instead of concentrating all his energy and will on his search, here he was once more involving himself in a conversation that did not really matter to him in the least. If he did not find Nélida—he understood this clearly now—life was finished for him.

XLIII

THE Salon Maguenta, a spacious room with vaguely Egyptian decor and a resolutely ochre color scheme, was almost empty that Tuesday night. Out of yellow amplifiers, strung on wires, music kept pouring, alternating between sweet and frantic. There was only one couple on the enormous dance floor. The other three or four customers were scattered about at small tables. When Vidal came up to the bar, he already knew Nélida was not there. The bartender was talking to a fat man, a fellow employee, perhaps, or possibly the owner. They continued their conversation, paying no heed to Vidal standing there, tense with expectation. *There are some slow-witted people who can see only what's right before their eyes, as though they were wearing blinders,* he thought angrily. But he suppressed the emotion, for, he reminded himself, he could not afford such luxuries. If he hoped to find Nélida, he would need everybody's cooperation. And to begin with, the good will of these two who continued talking, quite unperturbed.

"What about that group called *La Tradición?* Did you make a deal with them?"

"I told you I would, didn't I?"

"And they didn't kick?"

"Why the hell should they—a bunch of young kids like that? They ought to be paying us for letting them play here. Do you realize what this means to them in the way of free advertising?"

"But in the meantime, what are they supposed to live on?"

"We have to live too, don't we? Waiting on tables, lugging trays, while what do they do? Play the guitar. Which, after all, is what they enjoy."

There was a moment of silence. Vidal seized the opportunity to ask, "Tell me, please, does a trio called '*Los Porteñitos*' play here?"

"Saturdays, Sundays, and holidays."

"But not tonight?"

"Not tonight. Would you expect us to provide an orchestra for these bums?" The bartender waved his hand vaguely toward the tables and the dance floor.

Turning away from Vidal as if he no longer existed, the fat man commented, "We'll have to put the screws on '*Los Porteñitos*' too. It doesn't do for these artists, or so-called artists, to make too much money. Just for their own good. Otherwise they get spoiled."

"Would you by any chance know a girl named Nélida?"

"What's she like?"

"Medium height, chestnut hair."

"Like all of them," said the bartender.

"I know a girl named Nelly," said the fat man, "but she's a blonde. She works in a bakery shop."

"How could you expect me to remember all the women who come around here?" asked the bartender. "I'd go nuts. Believe me, they're all as alike as peas in a pod: dark-skinned, black-haired. One country girl after another, all spilling over into Buenos Aires."

If he didn't persist, he would never find her. Trying to sound off-hand, he said, "Try to remember, gentlemen. I'd be willing to bet you know her."

"I can't place her."

He tried once more, speaking very quickly, as though the words burned his tongue: "She was engaged to a fellow named Martín who plays in '*Los Porteñitos*.'"

"Martín," the fat man echoed, ponderously. "That's the guy

you're going to have to talk to."

"Don't worry," said the bartender. "I'll be seeing him Saturday."

"Where is The Corner Spot?"

They had stopped listening. But the fat man answered finally, "Not far. Just around the corner."

XLIV

THE Corner Spot was decorated completely in light colors, with white walls. Vidal took one quick glance, from the door. There was only one customer, a very thin man blowing on a cup he was holding in both hands. *No point asking here,* he decided, and set out again along Güemes. The entrance to FOB was by way of a rather cramped spiral stairway. The place looked like a coal-cellar, tiny and very dark. If Nélida were here, she would have plenty of time to get away before his eyes adjusted to the darkness. But was there any reason that she should want to avoid him? She had always been open in her dealings with him, but perhaps because he was a little desperate, he felt that love was an uncertain thing, that she could be easily turned against an imbecile like him, incapable of self-control, or of staying home and waiting, as they had agreed he should . . . Anyway, he deemed it wise to stay where he was until he had got used to the darkness. He stood there with his left hand on the stair rail, trying to make out the faces of the people. *I hope no one notices me and comes to show me to a table . . .* He was doubtlessly upset; when a hand was laid on his, his heart started beating violently. On the other side of the railing barely visible, a woman stood watching him. *Until my eyes get adjusted to the darkness, I can't tell who it is. Most likely it's Nélida. Please, let it be Nélida.* It was Tuna.

"What are you doing here? Come over and sit with me."

He followed her, seeing clearly now, as though the darkness had been dispelled.

"What'll you have?" the waiter asked.

"Do you mind?" said Tuna. "They always grouse if you don't order something. We'll leave right afterwards."

"Order anything you like."

He was certain that Nélida was not here. Should he tell the truth now, he wondered. But before he could decide, he heard himself saying, "I'm looking for a friend named Nélida."

"You're kidding."

"Why do you say that?"

"Oh, because. To begin with, it's sort of stupid. And besides . . ."

"I don't understand."

"What do you mean, you don't understand? You could get carried away for one minute and then spend the rest of your life regretting something rash."

"I'm not unbalanced."

"All right, so you're not. But a sensible man doesn't put himself on the spot that way. You may have the best of intentions, but if you find the girl in somebody's arms, you'll go off your rocker. It can happen."

"I don't think so."

"You don't think so, you don't think so. Why? The girl's a saint, maybe? If you ask around at places for her, nobody's going to be foolish enough to admit having seen her, even though she may have just left."

"But if you're looking for her because you love her?"

"Like the guy who scrawled 'Angélica, I'll find you yet' on the walls of Vilaseco's hotel? Look, people are cagey, they don't want to get involved. And they always side with the one who's trying to get away."

"I have to talk to a girl named Nélida, or else tó a fellow named Martín."

"Let them have their fun, and come along with me to the

little hotel in the next block. They provide every comfort. They even have background music."

"I can't, Tuna."

"You know, these days it's not wise to offend a young woman."

"I've no wish to offend you."

Tuna smiled. He patted her arm, paid the bill, and left.

XLV

He planned to go straight to the apartment on Guatemala Street. To strengthen this intention he told himself, *She may be waiting for me.* Then he envisioned the empty rooms, and decided he would stop first at his own apartment house to ask if Antonia could give him any news of Nélida. Though they had been together only a few short hours, he was already accustomed to the happiness of living with her. As he walked back along Güemes, the street seemed to stretch out interminably. The sidewalk was hard beneath his feet, and the cornices and the ornamentations of the dreary façades of the houses were depressing to look at. The thought of Nélida was a talisman against discouragement, but it also brought with it the fear that he had lost her. To distract himself, he thought of Tuna, and suddenly understood Rey's behavior the day he had tricked Vidal into meeting him at the hotel. Boys and old men alike boast of their conquests (because they already or still can get women). Rey had tried to involve him in the business with Tuna so that afterwards he would be in no position to make light of Rey's behavior. One of the few things life had taught him was that a person should never break up an old friendship just because he has discovered some pettiness or weakness in a friend. Living in the tenement he had discovered that people, no matter what hideous weakness they might display in their personal relations, were nonetheless capable of facing life and death with courage. He had learned too that fate was impartially just or unjust: there was no cause for him to feel pride, but rather only gratitude that he had found Nélida instead of Tuna.

So as to waste no time, he would not even go to his own room. If Isidorito saw him, he would detain him with questions—Where had he been? Why wasn't he staying?—and very likely they would end up having an argument. *What son is not exasperated by the sight of his own father in love, tagging along after a woman like a child? Of course, Nélida is different. Probably the poor boy is worried, thinking something may have happened to me. Although this loathing for old people may have infected him too. The other night, when he hid me in the attic, he must have been trying to protect me, but he treated me with a lack of respect that I won't tolerate.*

He fell silent when he got to the house, lest someone he knew should hear him. Cautiously he opened the door and went in. Perhaps because he had sneaked in like a thief, or because he had lived for a day at Nélida's, or because he himself had changed, it seemed to him that he noted a change in the appearance of the court. It looked dreary, as the house fronts had a few minutes before. All the houses he saw kept reminding him of others—seen where, he could not recall—with crude façades weighed down by heavy ornamentation. He must have seen them in a dream.

He crossed the first courtyard, knocked at the door, and waited. He heard a smothered voice inside the room saying over and over, "I'm the one in charge here, I'm the one in charge, I'm the one in charge." In his confusion he had knocked at *doña* Dalmacia's door. He knocked now at Antonia's. *If she hasn't seen Nélida,* he thought quickly, *she's going to think we've quarreled, no matter what I say. And if she has seen her, she's going to have bad news for me.* He didn't have the strength to stand bad news about Nélida.

"Oh, it's you. You'll have to excuse the way I look," said Antonia, smoothing her dress. "I had just laid down. How lucky that you showed up. Have you seen her?"

It seemed to him a good sign that Antonia's manner was so

easy and friendly. *It's because she and Nélida are so close,* he thought, *and now I'm part of Nélida.*

"No I haven't."

"You don't mean it. The poor girl must be half-crazy by this time. She went to the bakery, she looked up all those crazy old friends of yours, she even went to Néstor's and then to the hospital."

"I don't know where to look for her now."

"And meanwhile you've really got this place in an uproar. Everybody's out looking for you. Even Isidorito—and you know he's the kind who won't lift a finger for anybody—even he began to get worried and went out to see if he could find you."

"Did he go with Nélida?"

"No, everybody's on his own. I think she was going to one of Eladio's garages—not the one on Billinghurst, but the one on Azcuenaga. You know, across from the Recoleta cemetery, that he uses as a hideout for old men."

"I hate to think of her being alone on the streets."

"Ha, she knows how to take care of herself."

"I hope no harm comes to her on my account."

"You should have stayed in the apartment, as she asked you to."

XLVI

Turning the corner of Vicente López, he caught sight of the cupolas and angels above the wall of the cemetery and noted, to his annoyance, that tonight every house he saw reminded him of a tomb. The wall appeared to have been blown up, and the street was littered with rubble, clumps of earth, pieces of wood, fragments of crosses and statues. A short, flabby, pallid man with a surprisingly stubborn look about him, who was barely managing to hold a trembling little dog on a leash, spoke to him.

"Barbarians," he said, in a voice that trembled as much as the dog. "Did you hear the bombs? The first one went off right in the Old People's Home. And just see what the second one did. Think if we'd gotten here a couple of minutes earlier? Just imagine."

The little dog was sniffing the ground frantically. Without warning, Vidal felt as though the desolation of the cemetery were flooding through the breach in the wall and drowning all his senses. He had to close his eyes, like a man fighting off a fainting spell. Sorrow like this must be connected with some great misfortune. *But the strange thing about it,* he reflected, *is that the misfortune has not yet occurred.* He thought of Nélida and prayed: *Don't let anything happen to her.*

A red truck with white trim was standing at the curb. Vidal walked by, barely glancing at it, and went into the garage to look around for Eladio or his helper. He read the sign, "Keep Out, Employees Only," and at once forgot having read it, because in his weariness he was forgetting everything, as though he were dreaming. Outlined against the automobiles in the rear, a figure appeared, with its arms raised high. Dimly Vidal realized the voice was calling to him. "Old fellow!"

For a moment he took this for an accusation, then he recognized his son's voice. The boy, his arms still raised, was running toward him. *He seems glad to see me. How strange!* he observed without irony, and without the faintest suspicion that he would so soon regret the remark. Images blurred before his eyes. An enormous mass loomed up; he heard a howl of pain, then a crash of grinding metal and shattering glass which seemed as though it would never end. Then, in a moment of dead silence—the impact must have killed the engine—he understood what had happened: the truck had crushed Isidorito against the cars at the rear of the garage. At this point the sequence of events became confused in his mind, as if he were drunk. The scenes themselves were still vivid, but the order in which they had occurred was all jumbled. Something kept jerking his dazed mind back to a kind of scarecrow sprawled across the hood of an automobile.

The truck backed away, very slowly, very carefully. Vidal realized someone was speaking to him. It was the driver saying, with a grin that was almost pleasant, "Well, that's one less traitor."

If they spoke to him, he thought, he wouldn't be able to hear his son's groans or his breathing. Someone had thrown an arm over his shoulders and was saying, "Don't look." (He recognized Eladio's voice.) "Be brave."

Looking back over his shoulder he could see the vegetables which had spilled out of the truck lying on the floor of the garage, among pieces of broken glass and a spreading pool of blood.

XLVII

A Few Days Later

The friends were sunning themselves on a bench in the Plaza Las Heras.

"They're no longer afraid to show themselves, have you noticed?" Dante asked.

"That's right," said Jimmy. "The plaza is swarming with old people. I wouldn't say that it improves the place, but at least we have peace and order."

"I find the young people are much more respectful and much more considerate," said Arévalo. "As if . . ."

"It would be very unpleasant if they suddenly took it into their heads to attack us," said Dante.

"Do you know what a young fellow was telling me?" asked Jimmy. "That this war fell apart because it had no solid base to it."

"If you keep looking in the other direction when you speak to me," said Dante, "I can't understand you."

"And do you know why the whole thing flopped? Because it was really a necessary war, and because humanity is just too stupid."

"It's the young who have always been the idiots," Rey declared. "Or are we supposed to believe that there's wisdom in inexperience, and that we lose it later on?"

"No, not wisdom," said Arévalo, "but integrity. Youth has its virtues. For lack of time, or lack of experience, it hasn't acquired a taste for money . . ."

"An idiotic war," Rey pronounced, "in an idiotic world. Any nonentity could have you put out of commission, just by saying you were old."

"If you talk as though you had your mouth full, I can't understand a word," said Dante irritably.

Vidal was sitting next to Dante at the end of the bench. *Dante won't hear anything,* he thought, *and the others are absorbed in the conversation. I'll just slip off.* He turned away, stood up, escaped across the grass, and crossed the street. *I don't know what's wrong with me, but I can't stand them. I can't stand anything. And now, where am I supposed to be going?* he asked himself, as though he had a choice. Must he give up the idea of living with Nélida if he didn't cut himself off from his friends? Isidorito's death had completely crushed him . . . He had no spirit left for anything.

He noticed that a small boy was looking at him in wonder. "Don't be scared," he said. "I'm not crazy, it's just that I'm an old man and I talk to myself."

Going into his room, he thought that life would be intolerable except with Nélida. He would empty out a heap of useless things from his trunk, uninteresting trinkets he had kept only as reminders of times gone by, of his parents, his childhood, his first love affairs, and he would burn them without regret. He would save nothing except his good clothes (only his best things belonged there), and he would go to live once and for all in the apartment on Guatemala Street. With Nélida he would begin a new life, without any interfering memories. Not until this moment had he noticed his radio set. *So Isidorito had remembered at last.* At the sound of that name he fell into a reverie, as if he had confronted something incomprehensible.

There was a knock at the door. He was startled. Perhaps out of fear, perhaps out of anticipation for who it might be. It was Antonia.

"Are you going to go? You may not believe this, but she's still waiting. I wonder where she gets the patience."

"I haven't decided yet," he answered truthfully.

"Shall I tell you what I think? You're like a child playing games."

"Yes, my second childhood."

"Oh, it's a waste of time talking to you. I'm going for a walk." She paused and added, "With my boy friend."

Alone again, he thought, *Those two, uncle and nephew, are responsible for a lot of this. What am I going to do about it? Nothing.* Changing the subject he continued. *For people like us, the solution is a woman like Tuna. Not that Isidorito's death—* he bit his lips, then, having begun the sentence, went on distractedly—*not that it has made a pessimist of me. It's just that now I see things as they are. For a while a man is free to do as he pleases, but when he comes near to the limits life has set, it's no use for him to declare that he's going to be happy just because he has the good fortune to be loved.* With a feeling of bitterness he recalled a drunk he had seen once in the old grocery store at the corner of Bulnes and Paraguay, who had mockingly spoken of love in a barely audible voice, calling it an effeminite young boy's extravagance. Vidal thought of his father's last days. Though he never left his bedside, he had felt that his father sensed that he was alone, beyond reach. There was nothing more Vidal could do for him, except lie to him from time to time . . . Now it came to his own turn, and if he went back to Guatemala Street he would have to lie to Nélida and tell her everything would go on in the same way, that they were happy, that nothing wrong could happen to them, because they loved each other. He bit his lips again. Isidorito's doctor was right, you have to look at things as they are. He lighted the gas and put water on to boil for his *maté.*

XLVIII

THERE was hot water left over, so he used it to shave with. Lathering his face slowly, as if this were some kind of test, an examination he had to pass, he shaved with scrupulous care. He wiped off the last trace of soap, ran an inquiring hand across his face, and was satisfied. He changed his clothes, tidied up the room a little, threw his poncho around him, put out the light, picked up his keys, and went out.

He walked along quickly, intent only on his destination. As though it wanted to offer him a distraction, the street presently produced a surprise. Turning the corner at Salguero, he met Antonia and her boy friend. However, the boy friend was not Bogliolo's nephew, but Faber.

"Aren't you going to congratulate me?" Faber asked. His voice was nasal and high-pitched, and his grinning lips were moist with saliva.

"I congratulate you both," replied Vidal, without stopping. It made no difference to him, he thought, whether or not this couple made a revolting spectacle.

He had almost reached the apartment when some children hopping along the sidewalk blocked his way. "Wait just a minute," they said to him. "We're playing war correspondent. We'd like to know how you feel about the peace."

"But why are you hopping on one foot?"

"We've been wounded. Will you tell us what you think?"

"I don't have time now."

"Shall we wait?"

"Yes, wait for me."

He pushed open the little iron gate, crossed the garden, entered the building, and ran up the stairs. When she saw him, Nélida threw open her arms.

"At last!" she cried out, and burst into tears. "Why didn't you come? Was it on account of what happened? How terrible, my darling! Didn't you need me? If I'm unhappy, I want you near me. How you've suffered! Have you stopped loving me? I love you, you know that. I love you, I love you . . ."

She kept crying out, protesting, moaning, asking question after question, until he seized her in a firm grip, steered her inside, and laid her down on the bed.

"The door's open," she murmured.

"We'll close it afterwards."

XLIX

"I'M going to close the door now. Can you guess what I'm thinking? I hope they've seen us, so they'll know how much you love me."

"I'm hungry," he said.

"You kiss me as though you wanted to eat me up. I'll get dinner ready. Meanwhile, you have a nap."

He probably did not even hear the end of the sentence, for he fell asleep at once. As it happens in fairy tales, a feast was waiting for him when he wakened: the table was set with a cloth and napkins, two plates, dessert, red wine.

Watching him eat, Nélida exclaimed, "You've changed beyond recognition."

"What is it?"

"I don't quite know, you seem ready for anything."

"Does it displease you?"

"No, on the contrary. It's as if for the first time you were wholly here, with me. I feel now that I can really depend on you." But she had scarcely uttered the words when she became alarmed.

"You're not going out, are you?"

"Yes, there's something I have to do."

"You'll be back tonight?"

"If I can," he answered, kissing her.

"Take your poncho, it's turned chilly again."

The children were no longer there when he came out. He

found instead a group of young boys lined up in two rows, one along the houses and one along the curb. As he passed between them, he heard somebody humming a popular song:

"*The time for making hay is quickly past.*"

"We're done with all that, you know," Vidal told them, and went on his way.

At the cafe facing Plaza Las Heras his friends gave him a warm welcome. "Eladio is taking Néstor's place," Dante told him.

Even Jimmy had to admit that Vidal played a good game that night. As for the others, Jimmy was sharp as ever, Rey as greedy for olives and peanuts, Arévalo ironical, Dante slow and deaf, so that everything was back in order. And when Eladio said how much he enjoyed being part of a group like this, he was merely voicing the general feeling. But since Vidal's team was ahead after every round, the losers soon began to grumble about the luck the winners were having. They played until the small hours.

"Where are you going, Isidoro?" asked Rey.

"I don't know," Vidal answered, and he walked off resolutely into the night, because he wanted to go home alone.